DAWN OF VAMPIRES

E.J. KING

Sign up for E.J.'s Mailing List.

1
———

"You don't have to leave." Grayson's voice was soothingly calm in the dark.

I sat on the edge of his bed, rubbing sleep from my eyes. It had been a long night. After battling Liam's army and clearing the destruction from the mansion, I'd had to endure an emotionally taxing conversation with Grayson. He had admitted the truth about how we first met, almost a year earlier. He had compelled me to forget at the time, but he had grown tired of keeping that secret. Now, I knew everything.

I was still processing the meaning of his revelation and deciding exactly whether I should forgive him for lying to me and erasing my memories. But I had been too tired to even think about leaving, so we'd both agreed to a temporary truce and I had begrudgingly climbed into his bed, sleeping as close to the edge as I could. Now, I was awake and I had to face my new reality.

"I think I do have to leave," I said, keeping my back to him. If I caught even a glimpse of his smile, I would lose my determination.

"The sun isn't even up yet." He was amused by my stubbornness.

"No, but *I'm* up. No need to delay the inevitable." Still, I couldn't seem to make my body cooperate.

"As far as I'm concerned, you never have to leave, Isabel." His voice was still heavy with sleep, but the longing in his words was undeniable.

I finally turned to him, smiling faintly. "Uncle Jim would disagree."

"I'll talk to him," Grayson said, completely serious.

I laughed. "I don't think that's a good idea. Jim won't be receptive to a strange man suggesting I shack up with him in a creepy mansion." I flinched, remembering something else that Grayson had told me during his confession last night. "Did you say that Jim was the person that sent you to find me?"

"I did." He took in a deep breath, a habit from when he was still human. My eyes had adjusted to the dark and I could see his chest heave from the breath. "I knew Jim before I died and transitioned. Let's just say, I had a minor criminal record." His smirk was dazzling even in the dark. "He came by the mansion one night and told me he had a niece that he thought was in danger. He said she didn't know about the whole Hunter thing and she'd been involved in an accident he thought was caused by vampires. He knew about me, what I am. He figured if there was actual danger, I'd be better equipped to handle it than him."

"Uncle Jim knows about all of this?" I said, surprised even though I had long suspected that to be the case.

"I think you should let him tell you what he knows," Grayson said. He inched a hand over in the dark and placed it on my back. "Later, though. Please don't leave yet."

"Why do you want me to stay?' I said, voice quivering just a little.

His smile was the sexiest thing I had ever seen. "I remember making a promise to you last night and I'm a man who keeps my promises."

It took me a second to remember that promise and when I did, I blushed as an excited thrill ran over me. Before the battle with Liam, I had pulled away from Grayson's kiss, telling him that we could finish it later. He had given me that exact same sexy smile and had said that he was going to kiss every inch of my body later. My body thrummed just from the thought of his lips leaving blazing trails over my skin.

"You did make that promise," I agreed, not sure how I managed to speak. When I looked at Grayson, I was suddenly aware of how much older than me he was and, most certainly, how much more experienced. There was a reason he was such a good kisser.

Grayson must have sensed my apprehension, because his smile softened and he said, "I'm not going to hurt you, Jones."

"I know." My voice was a barely audible breath. "Okay, I'll stay."

He sat up abruptly and cupped my chin in his hand. "Thank you." His eyes searched mine for a moment, impossibly penetrating. I felt myself tremble slightly and his eyes registered surprise. "Isabel, do I frighten you?"

"No," I said with a hurried shake of my head. I was surprised at how easily I'd found that answer. "You just unsettle me. You're not like anyone I've ever known, Grayson."

"I hope that's a good thing," he said with a heart-breakingly sweet smile. "You should know, I'd be willing to change for you. I'll be anyone you want, as long as you'll agree to be with me."

"I don't want you to change," I said firmly. "You're so different when it's just the two of us. I like this version of you."

His hand stroked along my jaw and down my neck, his eyes still locked onto mine. "I like this version of me, too. I like the version of me that is enchanted by you."

No one had ever said anything like that to me. If Grayson hadn't been looking at me with such an open and vulnerable expression, I would have just assumed he was saying those words to get me to let him do anything he wanted. But Grayson didn't need to play games with me, and he knew it. I was just as enchanted by him as he was by me.

"Were you mad when I didn't follow you to the school last night?" I asked.

"Mad?" He shook his head. "I was worried, but I wasn't mad."

"Nick would've been mad," I whispered.

His eyes darkened slightly at Nick's name. "How many times do I have to tell you that I'm not Nick?"

"I didn't mean... I'm not..." I couldn't stop myself from being flustered under Grayson's unrelenting stare. I took a deep breath and started again. "I'm glad that you aren't him, Grayson. I love Nick. I probably always will, but we were doomed before we even really started because he always saw me as someone he had to protect. I was never an equal in our relationship."

"It's not bad that he wanted to protect you, Isabel," Grayson said carefully. "I would just rather make sure you can protect yourself."

"You sent him to take me to the dance," I said, finally

asking a question I had been wanting to ask him for hours. "Why?"

"I have a masochist streak," he said with a wry grin. "Believe me when I say that was not my favorite moment."

I narrowed my eyes. "Then why?"

"Because I didn't want you to go alone," he said with a simple shrug. "I wanted to be there with you, but you told me that wasn't what you wanted. I knew that you wanted to go with Nick. I thought it might make you happy."

I sucked in a breath. "You did it to make me happy?" I had just assumed he had sent Nick to keep an eye on me in case Liam made a move. It had never occurred to me that he had been aiming to give me a perfect teenage-girl night.

"Up until a few hours ago, I thought you were still madly in love with him," Grayson said softly. "You told me as much yourself."

"I was wrong." I remembered how hurt Nick had looked at the dance when I told him that I wasn't still in love with him. It had been so hard to say those words, but I didn't regret being honest about my feelings. "I wanted to be in love with Nick because he was the easy choice. I knew exactly how he felt about me and he was already such a big part of my life. It never occurred to me that I was settling for safe when I really wanted more."

"More? Like what?" Grayson's hand had trailed lazily from my neck to my side, slowly inching back the fabric of his t-shirt that I had worn to bed.

Feeling emboldened by his touch, I said, "Like passion. Like desire."

"Desire," he murmured back to me, hand sliding up my shirt. His mouth was so close to mine I could almost taste him. "If it's alright with you, I'd like to make good on my promise now, Isabel."

"I won't stop you," I said, my mouth parting in anticipation of his kiss.

His lips were softer than I remembered, but the hunger behind them was undeniable. It was matched only by the ferocity of his touch. He pulled the shirt over my head so smoothly I didn't even realize it was gone until I felt cold air on my skin. The cold air was quickly washed away by his fiery touch. I gasped as his hands stroked over my body. He had me laid flat on my back in one swooping motion.

Grayson pulled back slightly, adjusting himself over me and in a halting breath, I asked, "Did you mean it earlier when you said that you love me?"

"I would never lie about that," he said fiercely.

I wanted to say it back to him, to tell him that I loved him, too. But I couldn't. If I said those words now, it would be a lie. I had feelings for Grayson and thought that maybe someday I would love him, but I wasn't there yet. We both knew it. Grayson didn't need me to say it back to him. He wouldn't want me to say it if it wasn't true. He would wait, but he wouldn't pretend that his feelings didn't exist. He would love me even if I never loved him.

"Good," was all I said and then he was kissing me again.

I was lost in the warmth of his body, the perfection of his soft caresses, and the slow trail of kisses that moved over my body. It wasn't until Grayson stopped abruptly, his entire body rigid with his head turned toward the door, that I realized something was wrong.

"What is it?" I whispered, feeling terribly exposed.

In one quick movement, he snatched the t-shirt he had removed from me only moments earlier. "Put that on," he breathed, still watching the door.

I had only just pulled it over my quivering torso when the bedroom door flew open. Grayson was still hovering over me, his body mostly shielding me from view. That only made matters worse when I saw our intruder.

"Nick!" I had thought that he had gone back to his place after the fight. It had never occurred to me that he had stayed in the mansion. That had been a huge mistake on my part. Regardless, he had no right to barge into Grayson's room. "What are you doing?"

"You need to come with me, Iz," he said. I smoothed my hands over the shirt to make sure I was covered and Nick seemed to register for the first time that he had caught me in a compromising situation. If he had been listening to us with his supernatural ears, he would have already known exactly what he was about to interrupt. "Now."

Grayson tensed and looked to me for confirmation of whether I wanted him to step in. I gave a slight shake of my head.

"What's wrong, Nick?" I said, gently nudging Grayson's body away from mine.

"Mom just called. Something sounded off, but she wouldn't tell me anything. She just kept saying that I had to find you and bring you to the house." Nick's jaw worked back and forth as he tried to hold the fear out of his voice. "Come with me, please."

"Of course," I said, scrambling to my feet.

Grayson caught my arm. "I don't know if that's a good idea."

"Stay out of this, Parker," Nick growled.

"It's a trap, Rockson," Grayson retorted. "If you care about Isabel at all, you would never ask her to walk into it."

I shook Grayson's hand away. "I'm going," I said firmly. It was hard to sound too authoritative wearing nothing but one of Grayson's old t-shirts. "Sadie is my family, Grayson."

He let out a labored sigh and said, "Fine. We'll go."

I expected Nick to protest and say that he didn't want Grayson tagging along, but no argument came. That's when I realized that Nick was afraid. He didn't know what we would find at the house and he wanted us to have backup, even if that backup was Grayson.

Nick left the room so we could both get dressed. As I slipped on Trina's borrowed clothes, I caught Grayson sneaking a glance at me. I cocked my head questioningly, but he just smiled stiffly. Whatever he was thinking, he wouldn't say it out loud with Nick right outside the door.

We drove to the house in silence. I was sandwiched between the two of them in Nick's truck and every nerve in my body was on edge. I had never seen Nick this tense, not even when Dorian had cornered us in the barn. Grayson was slightly more relaxed, but I was sure that he was still upset we were even going. He was convinced it was a trap and I was convinced I didn't care.

"No signs of a disturbance," Grayson muttered when we were parked in front of the house. Sadie's car was in the driveway, but Jim's sheriff's cruiser was gone. He had most likely gone into work early.

"Feel free to stay in the truck," Nick hissed back.

"Both of you, stop." I bumped Grayson's shoulder, urging him out of the truck. It was like bumping against a stone wall, but he didn't resist.

I stayed close to Grayson, letting Nick take the lead. In the lowest voice possible, I said, "Do you hear anything?"

"I'm not sure. No voices, but there's a strange gurgling sound." He froze and his eyes widened. "I smell blood. Lots of it."

It must have hit Nick at the same time because he surged forward in a rush. I was right behind him while Grayson stayed a few steps back. No doubt he still thought we were running into a trap, but he didn't try to stop me.

I was running so close to Nick that I crashed into his back when he pulled up abruptly in the entryway to the kitchen. His entire body shuddered once and then he lurched forward, falling to his knees. A startled gasp escaped my lips at the sight of Sadie bleeding on the floor. Her neck had been torn open and she was breathing in gargling gasps. Nick put a hand over the wound and her eyes flew open.

"Isabel," she said, though her eyes were only on Nick.

"I'm here," I stepped into her line of sight and dropped down next to Nick.

"Oh good." She exhaled a hard breath that sent a spray of blood droplets into the air.

I was aware that Grayson was already calling for an ambulance, but I was desperate to do more to help her. She was losing so much blood.

"Isabel." Grayson hung up his phone and stooped across from me. "I might be able to help her."

I had heard the rumors about vampire blood having healing capabilities, but I had never seen it in action. According to the legend, the blood could temporarily strengthen a human, allowing them to survive injuries that might otherwise be fatal. But the legend also said that if the timing was off, Sadie could die with vampire blood in her system, turning her into a vampire. The questioning look Grayson gave me confirmed that the legend was true. His blood might heal Sadie, but it also might make her a vampire.

"He's coming for you, Isabel," Sadie whispered around a fit of bloody coughing.

I didn't have to ask her who was coming. The scene

before us could only be the work of an evil monster like Liam.

"Did he do this to you?" I asked, my head spinning. Grayson's hand on my shoulder kept me from tipping over.

Sadie tried to shake her head, but she only managed a slight twitch of her face. Nick's fingers were covered in her blood and his face was twisted in pain. He was fighting hard against the urge to drink Sadie's blood.

"Fix her, Grayson," I said, making the decision. She wasn't going to make it long enough for the ambulance to arrive. Nick looked at both of us, his eyes strangely blank.

"What are you going to do?" he asked, sounding lost.

He hadn't been a vampire long enough to know all the tricks. I was sure he had never heard of the legend about vampire blood. That meant he also didn't know about the risk, couldn't fully comprehend that I might have just sentenced his mother to an eternal life she would never want.

"Grayson's blood could heal her," I said. "Vampire blood has healing properties for some humans."

Before Nick could ask any further questions, Grayson bared his fangs and sank them into his wrist. A soft crunching noise was followed by a stream of blood. He held his wrist firmly over Sadie's open mouth. At first, she choked on the blood, but then she swallowed it down. I wasn't sure how much blood she needed to drink and how long it would take before we would see results, one way or the other.

It was too hard to watch, so I walked a few feet away and stared out the window. Nick was too tortured by the sight of the blood and he had to leave the room. When Grayson joined me at the window a minute later, the puncture marks on his arm were already healing. "It should take effect soon," he said, answering my unasked question.

"Liam did this to her," I said, bile rising in my throat. "He came after my friends first and now he's coming after my family."

"Isabel." He put a heavy hand on my shoulder. "This isn't your fault."

"I should've been here," I whispered heatedly. "Instead of in your bed. I should've been here to protect her."

Grayson's face turned paler than usual. My words were more effective than a knife to the heart. He had been the one to convince me to stay in his bed. I didn't expect him to respond, but very quietly he said, "I'm sorry, Isabel."

He didn't need to apologize. It wasn't his fault. Neither of us could have predicted Liam's next move. Even if we had, there was no guarantee that we would've been able to stop him in time. Anger rolled through my body as I stared at Sadie's bloody neck, her body now completely still.

With pure hatred in my voice, I said, "Liam is the one who is going to be sorry."

2

I was the one who had to call Jim and tell him to meet us at the hospital. Nick was in no condition to do much more than stare at the wall in front of him. Grayson's blood hadn't turned Sadie yet, but it was unclear if he had acted in time to save her. Doctors were working furiously and all we could do was wait.

I sat between Nick and Grayson on uncomfortable chairs in the waiting room. Grayson hovered his hand over my leg at least a dozen times but seemed to think better of actually touching me. No doubt he was still remembering my comment back at the house. Nick hadn't spoken once since we arrived at the hospital and I was worried he had gone into shock. When I noticed his hand shaking, I placed mine on top of it. I was surprised when he didn't pull away and instead thread his fingers through mine.

"I'm going to take a walk," Grayson said. He had to have noticed our intimate moment, but he was too self-assured to mention it. His hand brushed my leg slightly before he left as his way of letting me know that he wasn't upset, he was just giving us some space.

When he was gone, I said, "I'm sure Sadie is going to be fine."

"Maybe," Nick replied in a hollow voice.

"Jim should be here soon." I wasn't sure why I couldn't stop talking. I felt a desperate need to fill the silence, as if everything would be okay as long as I just kept talking. "He'll know what to do."

"Iz," Nick said, looking at me for the first time. His grip on my hand tightened. "There's nothing Jim can do."

"I know," I whispered. "I'm so sorry."

He gave a sharp shake of his head. "Don't apologize. This wasn't your fault. Liam did this."

"Because of me," I added.

"Because he's a monster," Nick clarified. He glanced toward the door of the waiting room. "You should go find Grayson."

"Grayson?" I flinched. "He's fine."

"He is, but you aren't. Let him comfort you." Nick offered the tiniest of smiles. "It's not my hand you want to be holding right now, Iz."

I felt a small crack run through my heart. Nick still knew me so well.

"I'll be right back," I said hesitantly.

He nodded and let go of my hand. "Go. I'll be fine."

I half-expected not to find Grayson. It was possible that leaving to take a walk had been an excuse to leave. I wouldn't have blamed him. Grayson didn't know Sadie and had no loyalty to Nick's mother. It had to be hard for him to watch as an outsider when there was nothing he could do and I was giving him the cold shoulder. But Grayson was only a few yards away from the waiting room and he wasn't alone.

He was talking sternly to Jim in a hushed voice. I was stunned to see them engaged in conversation like old friends. Grayson was clearly telling Jim something he didn't want to hear, but eventually he nodded his head. It was one thing to know that Grayson had helped Jim get me to Shaded Falls, but it was another thing completely to see Jim deferring to Grayson.

"Jim," I said loudly, interrupting their heated discussion.

"Any update?" he asked. There was so much pain and worry in his eyes that I wanted to throw my arms around him, but Jim and I never hugged.

I shook my head. "Not yet. Nick is still waiting in there." I gestured to the waiting room. "Is everything okay out here?"

Jim and Grayson exchanged a look. Grayson said, "Go on inside, Jim. I'll fill her in."

I waited for Jim to argue, but he just squeezed my arm gently and went into the waiting room. Grayson watched him disappear and held out his hand. "Let's take a walk."

Now, I realized that when Grayson had initially said he was taking a walk, he had actually heard Jim arrive and had left to sneak in a conversation with him. Grayson was always one step ahead of me. I took his hand and he sighed– he was relieved. He had been worried I was still blaming him.

"Thank you for coming with me," I said as we walked. It was not quite an apology, but it was close enough for Grayson.

"You don't have to thank me for that." He surprised me by dropping my hand and putting his arm around my shoulders. "She'll be alright, Isabel. My blood will help her heal."

"Thank you for helping her." I couldn't seem to stop thanking him.

He tightened his arm around me rather than reply. I was still getting used to Grayson. He was so much harder to understand than Nick. Nick wore his emotions on his sleeve and never tried to hide those emotions from me. Grayson was an enigma. His emotions were much deeper, hidden under a careful mask of calm.

"What were you telling Jim?" I said.

"I confirmed that it was a vampire attack and I told him that once Sadie recovers enough, he needs to take her away from Shaded Falls." Grayson's arm dropped away without resistance as I shrugged myself free.

"You told him to leave? What were you thinking?" I glared at him.

Grayson, as always, stayed calm. "It's the only thing we can do to guarantee your family's safety."

"He'll never leave without me, Grayson. He's going to make me leave with him. You get that, right?" My anger continued to flare. "You just sent *me* away."

"If you want to stay, I'll talk to Jim," Grayson said, still confused about why I was so angry.

"You really think Jim is going to let me stay if you tell him to?" I scoffed. "You really do think highly of yourself. You need to remember that Jim isn't one of your vampires."

He let out an exasperated sigh and threw up his hands. "What do you want from me, Isabel? I'm trying to keep your family safe. I'm trying to keep *you* safe. Just tell me what you want and I'll do it, but please stop looking for any little excuse to hate me."

"I don't hate you, Grayson," I mumbled like a petulant child. His scolding was completely deserved.

"What do you want from me?" he repeated, his voice breaking for the first time.

The weight of everything that had happened in the last 24 hours had been pressing down so hard that I felt like I was seconds away from crumbling. Elena had been kidnapped, Sloan and been compelled and turned against me, and Sadie had almost died. What I really wanted was to go back in time and prevent all those things, but that was something that could never happen.

"A hug?" I said in weak voice that was just on the edge of a sob.

Grayson's guarded face cracked and he smiled sadly. "Get over here."

I gladly fell into his embrace, crashing hard against his solid chest. His arms were like a protective shield around me. I closed my eyes and took measured breaths, deeply inhaling his intoxicating scent. It felt like a hug from Grayson could fix almost anything.

"I'll talk to Jim," I said, my face still buried in his chest. "I'll convince him that he needs to leave me behind when he takes Sadie away."

"You could go with him. I would understand." Grayson's tone was cautious. He was probably afraid I would snap at him again and ruin our tender moment.

"No, I need to stay. I need to fight." I tilted my head back to make eye contact with him. "Besides, I'm not sure I could leave you, even if I wanted to."

He smiled, looking almost boyishly shy as he added, "You should move into the mansion. It won't be safe for you in that house."

"You're asking me to move in?" I teased playfully. "That was fast."

"For your safety," he said quickly. "I'll make sure you have your own room."

I tilted my head. "That is going to make it hard for you to keep your promise."

He chuckled and his hand stroked slowly in a circular motion over my back. It created a swirl of heat across my skin. "You're always welcome in my bed, Isabel."

"We shouldn't do this here," I said, stepping back. We

were still in a public hospital hallway with nurses and patients bustling past us. Nick was in the waiting room, possibly still in supernatural-hearing distance. Jim could come into the hall at any second.

"You sure know how to kill a mood, Jones." Grayson's wall went back up. "I need to get back to the mansion and take care of some business."

"Of course. Go. I'll call you later." I sounded more confident than I felt.

Grayson stared hard at me, as if challenging me to admit that I didn't want him to leave. When I didn't relent from my own stubborn stare, he said, "Don't go back to the house alone. You don't have to go with me, but at least take Nick."

He left before I could respond.

I told myself that I was acting so hot and cold with Grayson because of everything that had happened in the last few hours. I wanted to believe that it nothing to do with being confused about my feelings. It was undeniable that my feelings for Grayson were different than anything I had experienced previously. A tiny spark in my brain flashed an answer that I didn't want to process. I forced that spark to extinguish and headed to the coffee machine. At least until I knew that Jim and Sadie were safely away from Shaded Falls, I wasn't going to think about the spark that Grayson caused.

When I rejoined Nick in the waiting room, Jim had been taken to see Sadie. The doctor had said she would make a full recovery and would be discharged the following morning. We were allowed to see Sadie, but she was under the influence of a lot of drugs and slept throughout our visit. Eventually, Jim convinced us to leave. I wanted to get to the house to clean up the blood before Jim had to see it, so I didn't put up a protest. There was nothing we could do for Sadie and she wasn't even aware we were there anyway.

Nick offered to help me with cleaning duties, and we spent a few hours scrubbing the entire kitchen with bleach. By the time we finished, it was night again.

"You're not staying here tonight, are you?" Nick said when I started toward my bedroom.

"I'm not sure Grayson will want me at the mansion," I admitted.

"Don't be an idiot, Iz. It's not a good look on you." He smirked. "Throw some of your things in a bag and I'll drive you over there."

"I need to shower," I said, glancing at the blood stains I'd gotten on my clothes when we found Sadie.

"Is that an invitation?" Nick teased with an exaggerated eyebrow waggle.

I rolled my eyes. "Our last co-ed shower didn't end so well."

A sudden cloud of dark washed over Nick's face as he remembered that last intimate moment we had spent together before he broke up with me. "I guess not," he said.

We took turns using the shower and headed to the mansion in clean clothes. The closer we got to Grayson's, the faster my heart thumped. I was both anxious to see him and also afraid of his reaction when he saw me. I hadn't called him like I said I would.

"He's going to be glad you came with me," Nick said when he noticed my anxiety. "Gray adores you, Iz. Even if you did treat him like crap today."

"You heard us?" I said.

"I can't exactly help it," he replied with a shrug. "Look, we both know I'm not Gray's biggest fan and I'm still hung up on you, but even I have to admit that you seem happy with him and it's more than obvious that he's smitten with you. Try not to hold your old relationship baggage against him."

Of course, Nick knew my past romances better than anyone. I'd told him about both Justin and Steve. He knew how I'd lost both of them and how I thought that I'd been in love with both of them only to realize later that my feelings weren't that deep. He knew how I'd thought I was in love with him, only to change my mind when I started having feelings for Grayson.

"He told me that he loves me," I admitted quietly as Nick parked his truck in front of the mansion. "I didn't say it back to him."

"You shouldn't, unless you mean it. If you don't want to be with him, let him go." Nick turned to me, his cheek twitching. "But don't deny the truth to yourself just because you don't want to get hurt again. You're not a coward, Iz."

I never expected Nick to be the one that would push me to admit my feelings for Grayson. My legs felt numb as I walked toward the mansion. Nick opened the door, letting himself in. I followed him into a room filled with vamps and hesitated in the doorway. Most of Grayson's clan had come around to me being in their home, especially after I had fought alongside them, but I still got more than a few annoyed stares. I was still a Hunter in a den of vampires.

"Isabel." Grayson's voice was so close behind me, it was like I could feel it on the back of my neck. He must have heard Nick and I arrive.

"Hey," I said lamely as I turned to face him. "I decided to just stop by instead of calling. Hope that's okay."

"Of course." He glanced around the room and noticed that a lot of the talking had stopped. "Let me take your bag," he said, reaching out for it.

I handed him the leather bag that was filled with some clothes and school books. He slipped it on his shoulder, eyes never leaving my face. I noticed the tiniest curl of his lips. He was pleased that I had packed an overnight bag, but he was trying not to let it show. Whether he was trying to hide that from me or the vampires, I couldn't tell.

"How is Sadie?" he said.

"She's going to be fine. They'll release her in the morning." I lowered my voice even though it wouldn't do any good. "Jim is staying with her in the hospital tonight."

He nodded, understanding. "I'll take your things to my room."

I could feel more eyes darting in our direction at those words. I remembered when one of the vampires, Beth, had told me that Grayson never invited anyone into his room. Now, I was practically moving in. Grayson disappeared down the hallway and I wished I had gone with him. Instead, I stood awkwardly along the wall and watched a dozen vampires talking like we hadn't just battled a powerful vampire and witch in that room just one night earlier.

"Hey," Grayson was back at my side. His hand brushed lightly over my arm, but he didn't let it linger. He nodded his head upward and gave me a hopeful look I smiled in understanding.

The first time Grayson had invited me to the house, he'd taken me up to a balcony on the third floor. It was the first time I had truly seen him as anything other than a cocky vampire clan leader and pseudo-ally in the supernatural war. We'd had a moment that had hinted at a possible future for us. Now, I was joining him on that balcony again, very much in the present.

"I'm sorry for how I behaved today," I said once we were seated on the balcony. Unlike last time, Grayson hadn't prepared the concrete floor with blankets and pillows. He hadn't expected me to come tonight. We sat a couple feet apart, our bodies angled toward each other. "The truth is, you unnerve me, Grayson."

"I've always been completely honest with you about my feelings for you, Isabel," he said, his gold eyes seeing me perfectly in the dark. "Even when you haven't given me the same courtesy."

"I haven't been keeping my feelings from you," I said. "I've been keeping them from myself. I don't want to have feelings for you. I'm not good with feelings."

"I've noticed," he said, lips twitching.

I frowned. "Glad that my emotional damage is entertaining to you."

"Everything about you is entertaining to me," he said. His eyes twinkled. "Do you have any idea how hard it is for me to stay focused on anything else when you are close to me?"

"I think I have some idea." I had been planning to say more to Grayson, but the words vanished when he smirked at me. Those lips… I ached to feel them on mine.

Grayson failed to read my mind, instead studying me for a long moment. "When I brought you up here the first time, I never imagined we'd end up where we are right now."

"Together?" I said, the word feeling unnatural on my lips.

"Are we?" he said.

"I've slept in your bed more than my own this weekend," I said with a small laugh. "I'd say we are together."

"We've been doing too much sleeping in that bed," he said, putting his hand on my neck, his long fingers threading into my hair.

That was normally the kind of statement that would make me blush and search for any excuse to change the subject. Not this time. I held his longing gaze. "I'm not tired at all right now."

I saw him glance at the concrete ground, contemplating. "I really should've been more prepared," he said with his sexy grin in place.

"You'll do better next time," I said.

He jumped to his feet, pulling me with him. "You're not getting off that easy, Jones."

Grayson forgot that I wasn't blessed with his supernatural speed and I had to hurry to keep up with his long strides.

"Slow down, Parker," I laughed. "We've got all night."

"I don't want to waste a second of it," he said seriously, turning to scoop me into his arms. It was so surprising that I just stared at him for several seconds.

"What are you doing?" I said as he continued to hurry down the stairs.

Grayson glanced at me. "Isn't it obvious? I'm romancing you."

I laughed and threw my arms around his neck. He carried my weight easily and didn't stop until we were on the other side of his bedroom door. When he set me on my feet, my legs felt wobbly. I had talked a big game on the balcony, but now my nerves were returning.

"You're shaking," Grayson said, putting his hand on my arm. He suddenly looked more afraid than me. "Isabel, you're not... I mean, is this... your first..."

"No," I said hurriedly, understanding what he couldn't quite seem to ask. This was not my first time technically, but in many ways it would be. Because I was about to do something I had never done– I was about to choose to follow my heart. "I've just never felt this way about someone when I've done it."

Grayson nodded slowly. "I get it. If it helps, I feel the same."

"That does help," I said, letting out the breath I had been holding. I closed my eyes and swallowed down the fear that had been rising inside me. "Please don't break my heart."

Grayson's arms went around me like a gentle blanket. He put his forehead against mine and waited until I opened my eyes. "I'll protect it with my life," he said, his eyes flashing impossibly bright, before sealing his promise with a kiss.

3

———

"Are you cold?" Grayson's voice sounded like a rumble under my head. I was lying on top of him, listening to a beating heart that would never skip a beat, unlike mine which had been fluttering like crazy all night. His hands continued to stroke my skin.

"That's not possible when you are touching me like that." I kissed his chest, letting my lips linger on his skin.

Despite his hurry to get to his bedroom, Grayson had taken his time with me. First, he had slowly peeled away every layer of my clothes, his eyes lingering on every inch of my skin. Next, his lips had followed that same slow and torturous path. My body had hummed in anticipation for what felt like hours before he finally released me from my delicious misery.

"Human skin is so warm," he muttered, mostly to himself. "My body must feel like ice to you. Are you sure you aren't cold?"

I lifted my head. "Are you really that desperate for me to cover up?"

His hand moved lower. "I'd be alright with us staying exactly like this for eternity, Isabel."

"Some of us don't have an eternity," I reminded him.

"We'll just have to make the most of the time we have." His hand moved up to stroke my cheek. His eyes were completely unguarded and it was the most vulnerable I had ever seen him. "Isabel, I want–"

He cut off so abruptly I worried for a second that I had gone deaf. But then I heard the howling.

"What is that?" I gasped.

Grayson gently rolled me away and sat up, keeping himself between me and the bedroom door. His eyes were wild with alarm.

"Shit. It's Dorian." He jumped to his feet and searched the room for his clothes that had been so carelessly discarded when I tore them from his body. He found my shirt first and threw it to me.

"Dorian?" I sat up and hugged the shirt over my chest. It was just in time, because the bedroom door flew open with a bang.

Dorian looked even more hulking than usual as he glared at us from the doorway. Grayson stepped to his left, doing his best to block me from Dorian. Grayson didn't seem to remember that he was still completely nude.

"Did I interrupt something?" Dorian asked with snarl.

"I will kill you," Grayson said, every muscle in his body tense.

"Simmer down, Parker." Dorian's eyes were still locked on whatever part of me he could see around Grayson's statuesque body. "I have to admit, this is an interesting twist. Seems like the Hunter will whore around with almost anyone in town. How does her blood taste?"

Grayson's punch was so sudden Dorian didn't even see it

coming. His head snapped back on impact. I expected him to attack Grayson, but Dorian just rolled his head slowly and smirked. "So, you haven't tasted her yet? Another surprise."

"What do you want, Dorian?" I interjected before Grayson could hit him a second time. I wasn't going to get worked up over any insults from Dorian. He wasn't worth the energy.

"You already know the answer to that, Jones," he said with a wink that made my skin crawl. He held up a hand as Grayson moved to hit him again. "Relax. Geez. I just need to talk to you, Parker. Put on some clothes and meet me in the other room."

"Talk about what?" Grayson said.

"Liam." Dorian turned and left the room as suddenly as he had arrived.

Grayson was already pulling on his clothes. "I really hate that guy," he said.

"Really? I couldn't tell?" I smiled despite the bubble of annoyance in my chest.

Grayson threw the rest of my clothes at me. "You're not as cute as you think you are, Jones."

"Yes, I am." I smiled sweetly at him before pulling on my pants. It was almost strange to be wearing clothes again. I looked up and Grayson was staring at me. "What?"

"Just taking one last look to store in my mental images," he said and his wink made me flush and reach for my shirt.

"How did Dorian get all the way to your bedroom without anyone noticing?" I said, pulling the shirt over my head. "Without *you* noticing?"

Grayson grimaced. "I was a little distracted, Isabel."

"Okay, were all the vampires in the mansion having amazing sex?" I challenged him.

"Probably not," he said with a reluctant smile that turned smug. "Amazing, huh?"

"Don't be gross." I rolled my eyes. "Let's go. The sooner we get this over with, the sooner we can get the furball out of the house."

Grayson laughed and threw an arm around me, kissing my cheek. "I think I like you, Isabel Jones."

"Like?" I said with a raised eyebrow. He shrugged, dropped his arm, and walked away, knowing that his silence would drive me crazy. He was right.

A dozen vampires and even more weres were gathered in the mansion's large meeting room. More weres were outside, howling loud enough to annoy even my human ears. I could tell from Grayson's grimace that he hated having so many weres in and around his house.

"I see you've brought friends," Grayson said through tight lips.

Dorian ignored him and looked at me. "I liked you better the other way," he said, eyeing my clothed body.

"I'd like you better dead," I replied.

Grayson was obviously annoyed, but he controlled his emotions and carefully stowed them behind a stoic expression. "Isabel, have a seat."

I gladly slumped into the chair next to where Grayson stood. Standing next to him had left me too exposed. In addition to the curious vampires, eager were eyes stared hard at me. I wondered which of them had been there the night in the barn when Dorian had tried to make Nick mate with me.

When I scanned the room, I didn't see Nick. It seemed impossible that he wouldn't be there given how many weres had showed up. I wondered if he had decided not to stay at the mansion. Maybe he'd gone back to the hospital to check on Sadie, or maybe he had decided to avoid overhearing any of my antics with Grayson. I blushed at that thought and Dorian grinned at me from across the table.

Grayson continued to survey the room until the last of the murmuring quieted down and people stopped looking at me like I was a prime piece of meat. When he was ready, he slid gracefully into the chair next to mine and folded his hands neatly on the table.

"Dorian, you've intruded into my home without invitation and infested it with a bunch of weres. Explain why I shouldn't kill you."

A few of the vampires snickered and many of the were snarled. Dorian leaned forward. "I heard what transpired here last night. You've lost many members of your clan recently, and all because of Liam. We have a common enemy."

"Why? What did he do to you?" I said.

Every eye turned to me and the vampire ones all looked surprised. Grayson's hands twitched and it occurred to me that I had spoken out of turn. Grayson was the vampire leader, I was just his girlfriend. I had no right to speak up at all, yet Grayson didn't admonish me. He wanted to hear Liam's answer.

"He and his buddy, Logan, have convinced half my pack to join forces with them. Liam is building an army to fight against us. We can't beat him alone, and neither can you." Dorian spread his hands on the table. "I got all the way to your bedroom door before you even realized it. I could've attacked you and your girlfriend before you could even untangle yourselves. I chose not to do that. I'm here to offer you a truce."

I was blushing so hard I thought my skin might burst into flames. Even Grayson seemed rattled as he let a long pause hang in the air. I had no idea if Dorian was being sincere. His story sounded good, but this was the same man that wanted to make me his werewolf bride.

"Your numbers are fewer than ours," Grayson said slowly. "You don't stand a chance against Liam's army on your own. It will be a difficult fight for my clan, but it's one that we could win. If we agree to fight with you, I need you to agree to some conditions."

"Go ahead," Dorian said.

"None of your weres must ever attack one of my vamps. If they do, they will be killed on the spot."

Dorian nodded. "I ask for the same from you in return."

"Assuming we defeat Liam, I determine what happens to any surviving members of his army." Grayson's eyes bore into Liam like lasers.

"Fine." Dorian nodded again. "Do we have a deal?"

"Not yet." Grayson paused, composing himself before saying, "You will not harm Isabel. Not tonight, not ever. You will not come around her. You will not threaten her."

The other two conditions had been so easy for Dorian. I was surprised when he hesitated on this one. He couldn't possibly want me enough to sacrifice the safety of his pack. His pause was long enough that several of the weres began to shift in their seats.

"I agree to your terms," Dorian said with one last glance at me.

"In that case, I dismiss the non-essentials from this meeting." Grayson sat back in his chair and all but four vampires stood. As they headed toward the door, Dorian waved a hand and the majority of his weres followed. I was so busy watching the activity that I didn't realize Grayson looking at me.

"Oh, sorry." I pushed back my chair. I almost expected

him to smile or squeeze my leg, but he just dismissed me with a tight nod of his head.

I left the room with as much dignity as I could muster, which wasn't a lot. Part of me was glad to be going back to Grayson's room alone. I was tired and had no chance of getting any sleep if he had been with me. I kept my clothes on and curled up in a ball in the middle of the giant bed. The sheets smelled like Grayson and it didn't take long to fall asleep. In my sleep, I dreamt of meeting Grayson for the first time, which meant I also dreamt of my father's murder. I knew it was a dream, but I still watched the whole scene play out before I could force myself to open my eyes.

I must have been out for a while, because Grayson was in bed next to me. His arm was around me and I turned slowly. I managed to face him without waking him up. Grayson was five years older than me, something that was usually quite evident. But when he was sleeping, he looked more like a young boy than a vampire overlord. His dark lashes fluttered slightly, a stark contrast against his flawless pale skin. Unable to stop myself, I softly ran my fingers over his cheek. When that didn't wake him, I moved my hand to his chest.

Grayson had saved me the night my father had been killed by vampires. He didn't even know me, but Jim has asked him to protect me, so he did. He'd been protecting me ever since, even though I had been oblivious. He had let me into his world, and into his home, without ever asking for anything in return. He had told me that he loved me without any expectation of hearing me say it back. In the last month, Grayson had devoted himself to me and I had done little more than whine about Nick breaking up with me and find any excuse to pick fights with Grayson.

The spark inside me was returning and this time, I didn't try to snuff it out. I needed to embrace that spark and be honest with myself about what it meant. "I love you, Grayson," I whispered into the dark, testing the words and enjoying how it felt to say them out loud.

Grayson's lips twitched into a smile, but his eyes remained closed. He was awake. I held my breath, waiting to see how he would respond. In a rumbling whisper, he said, "I love you, too, Isabel."

I exhaled in relief before leaning in to kiss his cheek. Then I tucked my head onto his chest and closed my eyes. His arm tightened around me, pulling me even closer. Tomorrow, we would deal with the fallout of Dorian's visit. We would plan how to fight off Liam. I would face Jim and somehow convince him to take Sadie away and leave me behind. I would fight for my friends, Elena and Sadie. But for tonight, we had each other, and that was enough.

4

"Don't forget. The test on Friday will cover the Revolutionary War all the way through the Civil War."

I stifled a yawn and pretended to be focused on my history book. Grayson had said I was crazy for going to school, but that was easy for a 23-year-old vampire to say. Besides, I could only spend so much time locked away in a vampire lair before I would go crazy.

The bell rang and I slammed my book shut and raced to the door. I had made it through all my classes and only had gym remaining. Normally, I dreaded gym because of the inevitability of seeing Dorian, but not today. Today, I wanted to see him. I had questions that only he could answer.

I changed into my gym clothes faster than ever and hurried out to the soccer field. We had moved from endless laps around the track to playing soccer. At least half the students on the field would've preferred to be sitting on the sidelines, but I enjoyed the chance to burn off some energy while also kicking the ball as if it were Liam's head.

When I spotted Dorian by the water coolers, I called for

a substitute and headed in his direction. He greeted me as always with a casual scan of my body that made me want to punch him. At least now the weather was cool enough that I was wearing pants and a sweatshirt.

"You just keep adding layers," Dorian said with shake of his head. "Pity."

"Cut the crap, Dorian. I need to ask you something." I crossed my arms and glared at him.

"Love to help, but I made a deal with your boyfriend. We're not allowed to talk, remember?" He cocked his head at me, obviously wanting to say more but choosing not to.

I rolled my eyes. "Since when do you keep promises? Let's be real, Dorian. I still think you're a complete scumbag, but we're allies now."

"Alright. I'll answer your question, but you've got to answer mine." He raised an eyebrow in challenge.

"Fine, whatever." I glanced around to make sure no one was close enough to hear. "Why didn't you team up with Liam? You obviously don't care about following any super-natural laws or being a decent person, so why not work with Liam to bring down Grayson? We all know you hate him."

"Did Parker tell you that we used to be friends, back when we were still human?" Dorian said. I nodded. "He found out that Kate and I had slept together and everything between us changed. We were fighting the night of the car accident. He confronted us about the affair and Kate lost her cool. She has a bad temper."

"What does this have to do with Liam?" I said, feeling angry that Dorian was telling me Grayson's story. If Grayson wanted me to know the details, he would have told me himself.

Dorian narrowed his eyes at me. "I don't hate Gray, but he does hate me. I'm happy to play the part of the villain, but

I'm also just trying to help my pack survive. If I side with Liam, I'll be under his control forever. My pack deserves better than that."

"Don't you think Nick deserved better than what you did to him?" I said.

"Nick made his choice." Dorian shrugged. "Isabel, I'm not going to apologize for trying to get you to join my pack. We're dying off. I'm desperate and I'm not going to hide that fact. You know that I could turn you right now if I really wanted to."

"You could die trying," I replied hotly. "And if I didn't kill you, Grayson certainly would."

A twitch of something human passed over his face. "Time for my question. How did that happen?"

"What?"

"You and Gray. Last I saw you, you and Rockson were practically betrothed. A month later, you're in Gray's bed. How did that happen?" He looked genuinely curious. "Is he that good in bed?"

Yes, I thought to myself, *he* is *that good in bed*. But I pushed that thought away. "Honestly, I don't know. Nick changed after the transition and Grayson was annoyingly good to me. I'm a sucker for men who aren't assholes, apparently."

"Guess that means I don't have a chance," Dorian said with a smirk. "Do me a favor and get lost before Gray sees us together. I'd like him to think I'm at least attempting to abide by the terms of our agreement."

"One more thing," I said stubbornly. "Have you heard anything about Liam keeping a human girl hostage? She would be my age. He took her at the dance Saturday night."

"I only heard about the witch girl," Dorian said, referencing Sloan. "But I'll ask around and see what I can find out."

"Thanks." I was surprised by the surge of gratitude I felt toward him. I'd never had any feelings for Dorian other than pure hatred. "Will you be at the mansion later?"

Dorian nodded. "I'll see you there, Jones."

When I left school, I was surprised not to find Grayson waiting for me. He had been meeting me there every day for the last month. I had become accustomed to seeing his cocky smile as he greeted me while leaning against my car. My heart dropped a little as I started to worry about what his absence might mean. Worse still, I wouldn't be able to find out yet. I needed to stop by Jim's house and say goodbye.

Jim protested leaving me behind in the falls for almost an hour. Sadie was resting in bed while he loaded their things into his car. I followed along, explaining in great detail why I needed to stay behind.

"It's not safe for you here, Iz," he said, slamming the trunk shut.

"I have to stay, Jim. I'm a Hunter, this is what we do." I tried to sound confident. "Besides, I have an entire clan of vampires backing me up. And weres, too."

"Where are you going to stay? At Nick's place?" Jim looked as uncomfortable as I felt.

"No. Nick and I broke up." I looked away. "I'll stay in Grayson's mansion."

Jim's eyes widened. "You're going to stay in a den of vampires? That's a terrible idea, Isabel."

"I'll be fine," I insisted.

"How in the world can you feel that way? Who is looking out for you there?" Jim was clearly oblivious to my relationship with Grayson. I would've liked to tell him under much different circumstances.

"Grayson is watching out for me," I said quietly. "He won't let anything happen to me."

Jim must have detected in my tone that I was keeping important information from him. Understanding passed over his face and he winced. "Grayson Parker? Really? It's like you are trying to drive me into an early grave, Iz."

"You trusted him to protect me before," I said pointedly. "Trust him now."

Those words did the trick. Jim reluctantly agreed to let me stay while he took Sadie someplace safe. He promised that he would come back to help me fight even after I tried to convince him to stay far, far away. Jim had never trained as a Hunter. His presence was going to be more of a liability than an asset. But he was also my uncle and guardian. He wasn't going to leave me to fight alone.

I visited with Sadie for a bit before leaving. She didn't remember a lot about the attack and Jim had convinced her that a human had done it. She thought they were just going away so she could feel safe and get some rest. I wasn't about to contradict that lie.

The mansion was bustling with activity when I arrived. In addition to the usual vampires, at least a dozen weres were also prowling around. I noticed that neither Grayson nor Dorian were among them. I found my friend, Beth, in the newly created weapons room and joined her at the table, helping sharpen the many blades in front of us.

"I didn't see you in the meeting room when the weres invaded last night," I said.

"I was busy," she replied vaguely. If vampires could blush, I was sure her cheeks would be bright red.

"Busy? Doing what?" I said with a laugh. Then I remembered what I had been busy doing when Dorian barged in. "Oh."

Beth wouldn't look at me, her fingers twitching over a knife.

"Who were you with?" I said, trying a different tactic.

"She was with me." Nick appeared next to Beth. "We were together."

"Oh," I repeated, gaping at them. I remembered how I had joked with Grayson about the other vampires not hearing the weres because they were having amazing sex. Apparently, I'd been right. "I didn't realize you two were... um... I see."

Nick nodded. "You're not the only one who moved on, Iz."

"Good, good." I turned away from him. "This is great news."

I liked Beth. I loved Nick, as a friend. The two of them oddly made a lot of sense. But that didn't mean I wanted to think too much about them being together.

"Isabel," Trina called from the doorway. "Grayson has asked for you to join us in the council meeting."

I froze as everyone looked at me. Hunters were not asked to join vampire council meetings. This was unprecedented.

"Okay, sure." I pushed away from the table and followed Trina down the hall. She marched straight into the meeting room while I hesitated in the doorway.

"Enter," Grayson said with a flick of his hand. He never even looked in my direction, keeping his eyes on the weres sitting across from him.

I glared at Grayson in annoyance, but I took a seat in the only empty chair at the table, which happened to be next to Dorian.

"Can I help you?" I said in an overly sweet voice that didn't match my glare.

"Tell me about Steve Grandwell," Grayson said, finally returning my stare.

"Steve?" I flinched. "What about him?"

Dorian said, "I've reached out to some connections in the were community to learn more about Liam. I've continued to hear about a Hunter named Steve Grandwell."

"Nick mentioned that you knew him," Grayson said in a harsh voice.

Nick must have been in this room before he had sidled up next to Beth in the weapons room. He had happily sold me out.

"Steve was my mentor. He taught me how to fight." I tried to keep my tone unemotional. "He was killed by vampires not long after my father's murder."

"He was a mentor?" Grayson questioned in a doubtful voice. "Are you sure that's all he was?"

"What the hell does that mean?" I said.

It was Grayson's turn to flinch. He had been implying something with his words, but it was something different than I had inferred.

"My connections suspected that Steve was actually working with Liam. According to them, Steve was sent to convince you to join Liam's clan," Dorian said. He had rightly interpreted that Grayson and I weren't able to have this conversation without our personal feelings getting in the way.

"That's not possible. Steve was a Hunter. He loved being a Hunter. He taught me how to kill vampires and he died protecting me from them. Why would he have done any of that if he was sympathetic to Liam?" I shook my head in disbelief.

Grayson leaned forward, at first sharing a look with Dorian before nodding and saying to me, "He fell for you,

Isabel. I'm sure he never expected that to happen, but he must have developed feelings for you and changed his mind about turning you over to Liam. That's why Liam sent his vampires to kill both of you."

"That's absurd," I said, even as I remembered that one night that Steve and I had spent together, when we'd both let our guards down.

"Is it?" Grayson said with a wry smirk.

"You didn't know Steve," I said firmly. "He only wanted to train me, he wasn't in love with me."

Grayson continued to study me, no doubt noticing the pink flush of my cheeks. "He didn't have to be in love with you to want to protect you from Liam. The real question is, why would he agree to help Liam to begin with?"

"How should I know?" I snapped. "If he really was lying to me as you claim, he wouldn't have told me his motives, would he?"

With an elaborate sigh, Grayson straightened. Dorian tried a different approach. "Did Steve ever tell you anything about his personal life that struck you as odd?"

"Like what?" I tried to remember if Steve had ever told me anything about his life before I met him. "We weren't exactly friends."

"You're completely useless, Jones," Dorian said.

Trina had been watching the entire exchange quietly, but now she spoke. "Does it really matter? This Steve guy was killed."

"I don't care about Steve," Grayson said in a near-growl. "I care about why Liam was using him to get to Isabel. I care about why Liam has tried multiple times to get her. I care about what he has planned for her."

With my eyes, I tried to tell Grayson to calm down. This kind of an outburst in front of the combined were and vampire council wasn't going to do him any favors. His personal feelings for me couldn't be what guided his decision-making for his clan.

"We should take a break," Dorian said, surprisingly being the voice of reason. "It will be dark soon and we still need to prep the squads on their missions for tonight."

Grayson nodded. "Trina, work with Dorian. Everyone else, please proceed with our previously discussed plan and report back as needed."

This time, I didn't wait for Grayson to dismiss me. I was the first one from the room. The chatter in the rest of the house had grown louder as the vamps and weres prepared for night to fall. I headed in the opposite direction, toward Grayson's bedroom. Once there, I stripped out of my gym clothes and dug through my bag for more appropriate hunting clothes.

"Nothing like walking into my bedroom and finding an almost naked woman," Grayson said from behind me.

"Don't get any ideas, Parker," I said, pulling on a pair of black jeans. "This is only temporary nudity."

"Like a knife in my heart," he joked. "We should talk about what happened in that meeting."

I pulled a gray long-sleeve t-shirt over my head and then flipped my hair free. Only now that I was clothed did I face Grayson. "Let's not, okay?"

"What weren't you telling me about Steve?" he said.

"Why don't you just ask Nick?" I snapped.

"It wasn't like that, Isabel." Grayson's eyes softened. "Nick came to us when he overheard Dorian talking about Steve's connection to Liam. He didn't tell us any details about your relationship with Steve and I don't really care about those details, Isabel. But you and I both know you weren't telling the full truth in there. I just want to know why."

I believed Grayson. He didn't care about my sexual history with Steve. Grayson never got hung up on that sort of thing, maybe because he'd already spent so much time watching me with Nick. "Steve had a brother. He never told me much about him, but his brother had been a Hunter, too. According to Steve, he was killed by a vampire."

"You sound unconvinced," Grayson said.

"I caught him on the phone one time. He didn't know I was there. I heard him talking about his brother and it sounded very much like his brother was still alive." I had almost forgotten about that phone call. "I never asked Steve why he lied to me."

"What if the brother wasn't killed? What if he was turned?" Grayson took two steps closer to me. "Do you remember his brother's name?"

I thought back, digging through deeply buried memories. "He called him Lee. I don't know if it was short for anything."

"Like Liam?" Grayson's eyes flashed.

I felt like I had been punched in the stomach. "It can't be."

"Are you sure?"

My mind flashed back to when Steve had told me about his brother. There had been a vagueness when he talked about Lee's death. I should have known he wasn't telling the full truth. I remembered his lectures about vampires and my duties as a Hunter. My focus should be on killing vampires that were feeding on innocent humans, he said. Other vampires weren't worth my time. I had never thought to ask him more about those other vampires. I remember that night when Steve had crawled into my bed. He had whispered that I was special and I stupidly thought he was confessing his love for me. I'd given him everything, including my heart.

The next morning he'd been in such a hurry to apologize. He regretted our night together. He regretted those things he'd said to me. Steve made sure he never got close to me again. Steve said our only focus should be on preparing me for what was coming. Now, it all made sense. Steve had been preparing me for meeting Liam. He'd been grooming me. Our one night together had been a slip. Steve was never supposed to get close to me. I was supposed to belong to his brother.

With a sudden lurch, I ran for the bathroom. I heaved into the toilet until my stomach was completely empty. How could I have been so stupid? How could I have trusted Steve? Maybe I was still recovering from my father's murder, but I still should've known better. I was stronger than that.

Grayson's hands skimmed my neck as he pulled my hair back. He didn't say anything at first, letting me catch my breath. Any dignity I'd had was long gone now. With a deep breath, I lifted my head and said, "If Steve wasn't already dead, I would kill him."

"You'd have to get in line," Grayson said. "You alright?"

"Yeah. I'll be fine." I dared a glance at him. "Sorry you had to see me puke."

"Me too," he said with a grin. "Pull yourself together, Jones. I'm leaving in ten minutes on patrol if you are up for an adventure."

"Sounds good." I waited until Grayson left the bathroom and then got to my feet. I flushed down my stomach contents and then splashed cold water on my face and brushed my teeth.

I felt almost normal when I rejoined Grayson in the bedroom. He was pacing in front of the bookcases.

"Are you sure you're up for this?" he asked in a concerned voice.

I pulled on my leather jacket and tucked a blade into my boot. "Just try to keep up with me, Parker."

When I straightened, Grayson was standing right in front of me. Our relationship was still so new that I couldn't read the look in his eyes. I could, however, feel my heart racing as a familiar warmth ran through me when he smiled.

"I kept up with you just fine last night, Jones," he said.

I grabbed his shirt and pulled him closer, planting my lips firmly against his. It was a good thing I'd remembered to brush my teeth because he returned the kiss eagerly, his tongue pressing hard against mine. Grayson never did anything with less than complete commitment, and kissing was no exception.

"You better work on that stamina," he said when I pulled away, gasping for breath.

"It's not really fair that you don't require oxygen," I said as my chest heaved. Grayson just smiled his sexy smile and kissed me softly. "Besides, I don't recall you complaining about my stamina last night."

"I have literally no complaints about last night." He ran a hand lightly over my neck. "Except for maybe how it ended."

I laughed as I remembered how Dorian had interrupted us, Grayson valiantly using his naked body to shield mine. "I think Dorian liked it though. He got a great look at you."

"Let's hope tonight he keeps his damn eyes away from my bedroom." Grayson let his hand drop away. "We should go. If we don't leave this bedroom now, I'll never force myself to leave."

"The bed will still be here when we get back," I said, giving him a playful smile. "Not that we need a bed."

"Isabel," he groaned. "You really have no idea hard it is for me to not ravage you right this second, do you?"

I gave him a gentle shove toward the door. "Later, Parker. Keep it in your pants."

"If that's going to happen, you need to take your hands off me." He looked purposefully at my hands which were planted firmly on his chest. I remembered how I had touched his bare chest last night and told him that I loved him. Grayson seemed to remember, too, because he smiled and put his hand on top of mine. "What you feel beating under your hand belongs completely to you, Isabel."

"I'll take good care of it," I promised, relishing its steady thumping. As long as that heart was beating, Grayson would be mine. Reluctantly, I pulled my hand away and turned toward the door. One of us had to be strong enough to walk away. Right now, that person would be me.

5

"I've got the others investigating the most likely spots were Liam and his pals might be hiding," Grayson said as we strolled outside. The sun had just set and I could hear wolves howling in the distance. "I figured you and I can take a different approach to patrolling."

"Different how?" I asked suspiciously.

Grayson took my hand. "We're going to hit downtown and see if any of the new vampires are passing themselves off as locals."

"You and I, taking a walk through downtown, holding hands..." I looked at him skeptically. "What's your angle, Parker?"

"I don't know what you mean," he replied smoothly.

"Don't play dumb, Grayson. You can't pull off that look," I scolded.

He laughed. "It's impressive how you complimented and insulted me at the same time. Nicely done."

"Just one of my many skills," I joked.

"Indeed." He squeezed my hand. "I overheard you talking to Beth earlier. And Nick."

"You heard that?" I winced. "Was I the only one oblivious to what was going on?"

Grayson laughed. "No, you're just the only one that doesn't have supernatural hearing giving you way too many personal details about your housemates."

"Ugh, everyone really does hear everything in that house," I frowned. "Everyone heard us, didn't they?"

"Probably not everyone," Grayson said sympathetically. "We mostly tune out the background noise otherwise it would drive us insane."

"But if they wanted to dial in, they could?"

He shrugged. "Sure."

"That doesn't bother you at all?" I glanced at him, marveling at his angled features under the moonlight. He still took my breath away.

"Why should it bother me? We weren't doing anything wrong, Isabel." He dropped my hand and put his arm around my waist. "Besides, neither of us were doing much talking."

His words didn't make me feel better. It wasn't exactly the talking I was worried about anyway. But it was obvious that Grayson just couldn't understand why I was so uncomfortable and I didn't feel like rehashing it with him. This was just one of many differences between us.

I noticed we had arrived in the downtown area of Shaded Falls. This was a part of town that I'd come to know well from my time dating Nick and hanging out with Elena and Sloan. It was strange to be there now with Grayson.

"This town is disgustingly sweet," I said, surveying a parade of pumpkins resting on haystacks lining the town square.

"They have to make up for all the monsters hiding in the shadows," Grayson said. He stepped closer to me to let a woman pushing a stroller pass by. She flashed him a friendly smile and he returned a slightly sadder one. "Humans really have no idea how lucky they are."

"You mean how vulnerable they are," I said, glancing over my shoulder and watching as the woman continued down the street. "In any other town, she could easily be attacked by one of those monsters."

Grayson fixed his eyes straight ahead and walked a little faster, dropping his arm from around me. Something I said had irked him. I caught his arm and pulled him to a stop. "What did I say?"

"It's nothing." He avoided looking at me. "I think sometimes you forget that I am one of those monsters."

"You're not a monster, Grayson." I lowered my voice as a group of teenagers drew closer to us. They had just left Hallihan's and were headed in the direction of the movie theater. Their carefree laughter cut an especially sharp contrast to our conversation. "Stop feeling sorry for yourself. It's such a turnoff."

"Excuse you?" He exaggerated hurt with a hand over his heart. "I thought you adored me."

"I did, back when you were a cocky vampire overlord. This mopey, pitiful version of you is not doing it for me." I shook my head in mock disgust.

The teenagers were almost upon us now and Grayson wasn't about to be mocked in front of them. He grabbed my shoulders and backed me hard against the brick wall of the courthouse. I gasped in surprise as he leered at me, the smallest appearance of fangs poking over his lower lip. "Still turned off?" he said as he retracted his fangs and gave me his famous sexy smile. I wanted to grab him and pull him to me, but he still had me pinned to the wall.

"Shut up and kiss me, Parker," I said.

I didn't have to ask twice. As he kissed me, he pressed his body against mine in a very purposeful way. I could hear the teens giggle as they walked by, embarrassed to have caught us in such an intimate moment. I couldn't have cared less. I doubted anything could have made me ask Grayson to stop. His kiss was just too intoxicating, his body too enticing.

He only broke away when a siren pierced the air. Sirens were rare in the falls and even more so now that Jim had left town. He only had a handful of deputies watching the town. As Grayson craned his neck in the direction of the siren, I sucked in hard breaths to clear the fog of desire from my brain.

"We should follow them," I said.

Grayson nodded. Even though his body ran cold, I always felt flushed when he pushed it against me. The second he pulled away, a chill enveloped me. He was already headed in the direction of the sirens. They had grown fainter to my ears, but Grayson could still hear them perfectly. He might also be able to hear what had drawn the sirens.

"Hear anything?" I asked.

He nodded. "Dead body, or maybe bodies. There's a lot of background noise and it's hard to pull out the details."

"We're getting closer," I offered as futile consolation. Grayson walked a step ahead of me, doing his best to control his supernatural speed so that I could keep pace with him. I wondered how much of his time spent with me required him to rein in his powers. Grayson was a pure vampire because his transition was caused by magic, not by vampire blood. He was stronger than other vampires and I was sure I hadn't seen the full breadth of that strength and power yet.

"They aren't going to let us get close," Grayson said as the flashing lights of a police car and ambulance came into view.

We had moved away from downtown and were on a residential street.

"We'll get close enough," I said.

Two police officers were standing on the porch of a yellow two-story house. They were talking loudly and gesturing with wild hands, but I couldn't make out their words. Grayson was having no trouble understanding them.

"Do you know someone named Gwen Baker?" he said, head tilted as he continued to listen to the cops even as he was talking to me.

"Sure, she's in a few of my classes. Cheerleader. Pretty girl." I felt the dread gnawing in my stomach. "Why?"

"She's dead," he said simply. "Her and two more girls. Attacked in Gwen's bedroom."

My hand closed into a fist. "Attacked?"

"Sounds like a vamp attack," he said, closing his eyes to create more focus. "Neck wounds and lots of spilled blood. There are signs that there was a fourth girl in the room, but no one has been able to find her."

"Would Liam have kidnapped another girl?" I wondered out loud. He had already taken Elena, so I knew he was capable of such antics.

Grayson shook his head slowly before opening his eyes. "I don't think so. I think that maybe Elena did this."

"Elena?" I blinked hard. "How? Why?"

"I think Liam turned Elena and is using her to distract you." Grayson gripped my arm. "Elena is a vampire that isn't affected by the magic in this town. It's possible Liam used Sloan's powers to make Elena invincible. I don't know for sure and it doesn't really matter. What I do know is that we have to stop Elena before she kills again."

"Stop her? You mean kill her?" I jerked my arm away.

"Elena is my friend, Grayson. She only got involved in all this because of me. Liam took her because of me."

Grayson stayed calm. "We don't have a choice, Isabel. She just killed three girls. How can we let her live?"

"I don't know. We talk to her and explain that there's a different way to live. We give her a chance to change, Grayson." I gave him an imploring look. "Is that really too much to ask?"

"Until we stop her, our entire existence is threatened. Can you understand that?" Grayson looked at me with cold eyes. "The death of three teenage girls is going to draw the wrong kind of attention to Shaded Falls."

"Is that all you care about? Yourself? Your clan?" I felt my throat tightening as anger boiled in my chest.

"Yes, actually," Grayson said without hesitating. "My duty is to the clan, Isabel. You know that, so please stop looking at me like a wounded puppy."

I sucked in a sharp breath. Grayson had never spoken to me like that. "Sorry, I just thought that maybe you also cared about me. My mistake."

Regret flashed through his eyes, but it was too late. I spun away from him and hurried down the street. Grayson caught up with me in a few long strides.

"Isabel, wait. I'm sorry." He reached for my arm again, but I dodged his attempt.

"It's too late for that," I said.

"Stop, please." He appeared in front of me in a flash of motion. I cursed his supernatural speed as I halted abruptly to prevent myself from crashing into him. "Of course, I care about you, Isabel. That's not even a question. I care about you more than anyone else in the world."

I took a step to move around him, but he slid in front of me. "Grayson, stop. I don't want to talk to you right now."

"I love you," he said with overwhelming urgency. "But that doesn't change my loyalty to the clan."

"I know." I had been avoiding eye contact, but now I looked at him. I could see the love in his eyes and that made it even harder to say, "I just don't know which is stronger – your love or your loyalty."

Grayson continued to stare at me with eyes that penetrated straight to my soul. But he couldn't answer my question. Most likely, he didn't know the answer. His loyalty had never been tested. Neither had his love.

"I need to find Elena," I said.

"At least we agree on that," he said with a hard edge on his voice.

"Can I trust you not to kill her on sight if I let you tag along?" I challenged.

He smirked. "Let me tag along? Fine, I promise that I'll let you make the first move when we find her."

"Such a gentleman." I glanced up and down the street, trying to get my bearings. I had a feeling that I knew where Elena might have gone if she was looking for more easy victims. "Which way is Elm Street?"

"Two blocks east," Grayson said, pointing to his left.

I started in that direction without giving him an explanation. If Elena was looking for maximum victim impact, Gwen's sleepover was just a warmup.

"Planning on telling me where we are headed or are you not talking to me?" Grayson said.

"Elena wasn't friends with Gwen. She crashed that sleepover," I said. "My guess is she overheard them talking about it last week before she was turned. She also would've heard about the gathering taking place tonight at the old campground."

"Then why are we headed to Elm Street?" Grayson said.

"Because it's closer than the mansion and we need a ride." I veered through a yard taking a shortcut to the diner. "Wait out here. I'll be right back."

I took the steps to Nick's apartment two at a time. I knew he wouldn't be home and that he kept a key hidden in a flowerpot. I found the key and let myself inside, marching straight to where he kept the key for his motorcycle. Nick would be annoyed when he found out I had taken it without asking, but that was a risk I had to take. We didn't have time to waste tonight.

"You know how to drive one of these things?" I said when I found Grayson waiting by Nick's bike. He had rightfully guessed my plan while I was gone.

"Yeah, sure." Grayson caught the key when I tossed it to him. "Rockson isn't going to be happy about this."

"He'll get over it." I gestured. "Let's go, Parker."

He climbed on the bike and got the engine started while I settled in behind him. I had forgotten to grab a helmet from the apartment, but I trusted Grayson's supernatural reflexes to keep us from crashing.

"You ready?" he said.

I tightened an arm around his waist. "Go."

The engine revved and we rocketed onto the road. Grayson drove faster than Nick and my heart seemed to be racing even faster. I squeezed my legs tighter around Grayson's hips as he accelerated through a sharp curve in the road.

"Trying to kill me?" I yelled into his ear.

"You need to learn to trust me," he yelled back.

We made it to the old campground in record time. I had only been there once before, right when I arrived in Shaded Falls. Nick had brought me. Being there with Grayson was going to be an entirely different experience.

He parked the bike and switched off the engine. I released the crushing grip I had on him and climbed off. Grayson smirked at me as I shook the tightness out of my arms.

"You're a nervous passenger," he said.

"Only when my driver is a psychotic vampire with a death wish," I snapped back.

"I wouldn't have let anything bad happen to you, darling," he said, still smiling slyly. He liked seeing me vulnerable.

I glared. "Don't try to charm me. We both need to be focused."

"There's a lot of kids here for a school night," Grayson said. He wrinkled his nose. "And a lot of sexual frustration."

"Well, they *are* high school kids," I said. "Comes with the territory."

"Does it?" He raised an eyebrow at me and smirked.

"Didn't I tell you to stop it?" I forced a glare even though he looked adorable. Grayson had an annoying habit of charming me at the exact same time that he was pissing me off. I gave my head an angry shake and started in the direction of the party.

Grayson walked easily alongside me. "You should try not to look so hostile. People are going to notice."

"So?" I flinched when his hand grazed against mine.

"Isabel, this is a party. Try acting like you want to be here so people don't pay attention to us," he said.

I had to admit that it was good advice. If I stormed into the party as a bundle of fury, it wouldn't take long for people to comment on it. If they commented on it, Elena would hear them and know I was there hunting for her.

"Point taken." I held out my hand. "Ready to act like a couple in love?"

Grayson laughed and snaked an arm around me, sliding his hand into the back pocket of my jeans. "We've got to make this look real, darling."

"Ugh." When he called me darling, my heart thumped happily. I hated that. I wanted to still be mad at him for our earlier argument. I didn't want to enjoy the way his hand curved around my ass. I really didn't want to smile when he kissed my cheek, but I found myself doing exactly that. "This is a temporary truce, Parker," I whispered to him, but it was too late. He'd already seen my smile.

We walked through the party, subtly scanning the area for any signs of Elena. She was nowhere to be found near the campfire or by the keg. We would need to check each cabin to make sure she hadn't already secluded her victims.

"I don't hear her," Grayson whispered into my ear. To the teenagers we passed, he and I looked like nothing more than a couple sneaking off to the cabins to hook up. Under different circumstances, that might have been a real possibility. "Wait."

I stopped short in front of the second-to-last cabin as Grayson paused to listen closer to whatever he'd heard. Before he could pinpoint the noise, I saw a shadow move in front of a cabin window. There was nothing distinguishing about the shadow, but I still recognized it.

I punched Grayson's arm to get his attention, probably harder than was necessary. I jerked my head toward the cabin and he nodded his understanding. The look he gave me said that he didn't appreciate my jab, but he fell into step behind me. As the leader of his clan, it had to bother Grayson not to be the one taking the lead. But he made no attempt to convince me to step aside.

After retrieving my knife from my boot, I climbed the three rotting steps to the cabin, praying with each step that I wouldn't make any noise. I could now hear voices inside the cabin, but not well enough to make out the words. Grayson dropped a hand on my shoulder and I looked at him expectantly.

He mouthed one name– Logan.

I was an idiot not to realize earlier that Logan was involved. Besides being Liam's most devoted follower, Logan was also Elena's brother. Logan also knew about Sloan's abilities as he'd been on the receiving end of them. It just so happened that Logan also hated me.

Until now, the voices had been muffled and hushed, but now a loud yelp slipped through the ajar door. I was done waiting. With a firm kick, I sent the door flying into the cabin. I hurried in after it, fully prepared to stab anything that moved toward me in the dark space. I was surprised to find Elena standing in the middle of the room, looking at me with frightened eyes. Human eyes.

"There she is," Logan grinned at me from behind Elena. "And you thought she wasn't going to show, sis."

"I guess now we know who's going to win the World's Worst Brother award," I said, trying to look strong and confident for Elena's benefit. "Where's your buddy Liam?"

"You could say this is a secret mission." Logan's eyes burned with hatred. "Liam has made it clear that his plans involve you, Isabel Jones. I'm going to be the one that brings you to him."

I expected to hear Grayson snarl or growl or make some other possessive male noise, but he was completely quiet. I almost turned around to make sure he was there, except I could see Elena glancing nervously at him.

"You didn't learn your lesson the last time you tried to put your hands on me?" I asked, stalling until I could come up with a plan. It was clear that Logan was willing to kill and use his sister as bait to get what he wanted. What wasn't clear was whether he would be willing to kill his sister.

"Your witch is on our side now," Logan said. He stepped forward into a ray of moonlight that was streaming through the rotting boards overhead. I could see that in addition to the hate in his eyes, there was an undercurrent of anxiety. He wasn't as confident in his plan as he wanted me to believe.

"That was a neat trick, compelling Sloan to do your evil bidding. You better hope Liam did that compulsion right or she might turn on you." I had no real clue how compulsion worked, but I assumed that Logan was just as clueless. "I wonder what it would feel like to be fried from the inside."

"If you keep resisting Liam, maybe you'll find out," he replied with a snarl. "What's wrong with your boyfriend? Is he only allowed to speak when you let him?"

My fingers tightened around the knife blade. "Lucky for you, I've already given him permission to kill you."

I heard the slightest shuffle of Grayson's feet. I could picture the smirk on his face and I almost smiled, but the fear in Elena's eyes brought me back.

"Can we get this over with? I'm bored." I twirled the knife, carefully studying every tiny twitch of Logan's muscles. Even with my hawkish staring, Logan's move took me by surprise.

He had Elena by the throat before she could even gasp. I took a step forward and he growled, "Don't even think about it."

"Alright." I took a step back, bumping into Grayson. "Don't hurt her. You don't want to hurt your sister."

"I'm a vampire, Isabel. All I want to do is hurt people." His look was pure animal now. "Why do you even care? She's nothing to you."

"She's my friend," I said through clenched teeth.

Logan laughed. "Are you willing to sacrifice yourself to save your friend?"

Grayson's hand rested lightly on my lower back. He knew that I would absolutely sacrifice myself if it meant saving Elena, and he wasn't about to let that happen. I wanted to shove his hand away, but that would give Logan too much satisfaction.

"Is this your master plan? Trading Elena for me?" I forced a dry laugh. "Grayson will kill you before he lets that happen."

"I don't think your boyfriend will do anything that might put you at risk," Logan said with a challenging look at Grayson.

Calmly, he said, "Try me."

Elena whimpered as Logan snarled, baring his fangs. His eyes were on me. "Liam claims there is something special about your blood. I can't wait to taste it for myself."

"Isabel is never going with you," Grayson said. He had edged alongside me now, apparently no longer willing to defer to a Hunter. "She'll never belong to Liam."

"Good to see you're not completely whipped, Parker." Logan was studying me for any reaction, but I managed to keep my annoyance hidden. I couldn't have expected Grayson to stay quiet much longer. That went completely against his nature.

"If you stop this now, I promise to make your death quick," Grayson said. His head was inclined almost imperceptibly. "If not, I'll let the weres tear you apart."

Weres? I shot Grayson a surprised look. He must be able to hear them outside the cabin. The fire in Logan's eyes had faded. He had been so focused on his plan that he had missed the arrival of the weres, until now. We were in the woods, so it made sense that wolves had been prowling around. I was less clear how they had known to come into the campgrounds, but I could worry about that later.

"Even if you make it out of this cabin, you aren't getting out of here alive." Grayson was back to being the leader that he always was, supremely confident and sure that he was going to win the standoff. But he missed the acceptance that had passed over Logan's face. I didn't, but I wasn't fast enough.

Logan sank his fangs hard into Elena's neck, tearing into flesh and muscle. He wasn't trying to drink her blood, he was trying to kill her. Judging from the gaping hole in her neck and the erupting blood, he was going to be successful.

I threw myself at him anyway, yanking him away from Elena. Grayson caught her before she could hit the ground. I knew that he would try to save her, but I doubted he would be successful. Her injury was too severe. With that thought, I swung my blade at Logan's chest. He caught my hand and twisted my arm painfully behind my back. The knife fell from my hand and I cursed myself for getting taken so easily.

Logan snapped his fangs toward my neck and I put my free hand flat against his chest, pushing with all my might. Something strange happened next. Logan was a pure vampire, like Grayson, and he was stronger than me. But my touch seemed to paralyze him. He stared at me, confused. My hand felt warm against his chest, like I was touching a hot furnace. His mouth opened in a silent scream as I burned him from the inside out.

6

———

Grayson was behind Logan and couldn't see what was happening. He reacted on instinct when he saw Logan's fangs just inches away from my neck, slamming a knife through his back and piercing his heart. Logan was already dead, but Grayson didn't know that. He tossed the dead vampire's body to the ground and gave me a once-over.

"You alright?"

I nodded. "What about Elena?"

"I'm sorry, there was nothing I could do." He reached out a hand to me, but I jerked mine away. It was still burning from whatever energy had allowed me to kill Logan with my bare hand and I didn't want to risk hurting Grayson. Hurt flashed in Grayson's eyes. He said, "Stay in here. I'll go deal with the weres."

I was already kneeling next to Elena's body. Grayson dropped a hand on my shoulder, offering a gentle squeeze before leaving me alone with her. This whole thing was becoming far too familiar to me, watching someone I loved getting attacked by a vampire and not being able to save them. First Justin, then my father, then Steve, then Sadie, and now Elena. Vampires had taken so much from me that it was almost inconceivable that I could actually be in love with one of them. Was I fooling myself? Could Grayson really be so different from the other vampires?

I shook my head to clear that thought and folded Elena's arms over her body. She didn't deserve to die like this. She had been a kind girl and her biggest mistake had been befriending me. Logan's corpse had decomposed already and I had to step over it to get outside. Grayson and the weres were meeting behind the cabin, close to the woods. No one from the party would go back that way, so they could speak without fear of being interrupted. I approached the back of the cabin hesitantly, not sure exactly what I would find.

"You should get her out of here," Dorian was saying. "Liam might be lurking around."

Three weres circled Dorian and Grayson in wolf form, their yellow eyes flashing hungrily. Only Dorian had transitioned back into a human, standing unabashedly naked as he spoke. I kept my eyes on Grayson.

"Liam isn't here," I said.

The look Grayson flashed me said he had been hoping I would stay inside, but he also wasn't surprised that I hadn't listened to him.

"How can you be so sure?" Dorian demanded, standing far too close to me for my liking. Grayson seemed to agree, because he edged himself between us.

"Liam wants me alive. He never would've sent a goon like Logan to gather up his prized possession." I looked only at Dorian's face, even as he waved a hand at his side. I would never give him the satisfaction of looking down. "You can understand that."

He smirked. "Indeed, I can. The question remains, why is Liam so hung up on you? You're not that hot, Jones."

"How should I know? You're the expert in Hunter fetishes," I reminded him.

"My fetish is purely about preserving the pure were bloodline. As a vamp, Liam can't procreate. His motive inherently must be different than mine." Dorian wasn't at all ashamed of his attempt to turn me into a were, even standing in front of Grayson who was growing more and more agitated, despite his efforts to hide it. "He said something about your blood. What was he referencing?"

Grayson was done humoring him. "We're not going to discuss this here. Logan has been neutralized. We can convene back at the mansion."

"Always on your turf, huh?" Dorian said with narrowed eyes.

"The last time we were on your turf, you threatened to mate with my girlfriend," Grayson growled. It was the first time he'd ever referred to me as his girlfriend and I almost smiled. "Let's go, Isabel."

As much as I wanted to storm off with him, leaving an irate Dorian behind, I couldn't. "Grayson, we can't just leave Elena in there," I said.

"We have to." Grayson grimaced. "We can't be caught here. Your uncle isn't in charge of things right now."

"I know. Just...her family needs some closure. They're already going to be in the dark about what happened to Logan, with no body to bury. We can at least give them Elena." I looked toward the cabin and felt tears prickling my eyes.

Grayson looked at Dorian. "Can you take care of it?"

Surprisingly, he nodded. "I'll make sure she's found."

"Thank you," I said, feeling a strange kinship toward

Dorian in that moment. He almost looked sad about Elena's death and I wondered if it was an involuntary, latent human reaction, or if he wasn't as evil as I'd assumed all along.

I followed Grayson to the parking lot, falling behind as I failed to match his long strides. We had stuck to the edge of the woods, so we didn't have to put on a show for the party-goers. I was glad to be alone with my thoughts. Had that moment with Logan really happened? My hand was no longer burning and I couldn't conjure the heat no matter how much I concentrated. Given that I'd never done anything like that before, it was entirely possible I had hallu-cinated the whole thing.

"Isabel? Are you getting on?"

I blinked and stared blankly at Grayson. We were at Nick's motorcycle and Grayson had already climbed on and revved the engine. I slid on behind Grayson and wrapped both arms around his waist, resting my head in the curve of his neck. He stroked a hand gently over my leg, under-standing that I was still thinking about Elena. He drove slowly on the way back to the mansion, but I held on to him as if my life depended on it.

The slow drive gave me a chance to clear my head and by the time Grayson stopped the bike, I was embarrassed by my clingy behavior. I practically threw myself off the bike and marched straight toward the house.

"Isabel, what the hell?" Grayson came up behind me, looking annoyed.

I ignored him, heading straight from the entryway to the kitchen. Grayson followed just a step behind, but he didn't try to stop me. He watched as I grabbed a bottle of whiskey and poured a few ounces into a glass. I gulped it down and refilled it.

"Damn," he muttered.

I was glad that the kitchen was empty, save for us. It wouldn't have been good for the other vamps to see my meltdown.

"Something is wrong with me," I hissed in a whisper.

"What?" Grayson's head snapped back. "What do you mean?"

"I did something, back in the cabin. Something happened to Logan." I held my hand in front of me, trying to make it burn. I couldn't explain it to Grayson, I needed to show him.

Grayson was looking at me like I'd gone crazy. "I killed Logan, that's all."

"No." I pressed my lips together. I had already said too much. "Not here."

He finally reached out a hand, but I dodged him, taking the whiskey with me as I navigated my way to his bedroom. Remembering a trick he had taught me, I headed into the bathroom and turned on the shower. I took another sip of whiskey and handed the glass to him. Grayson gave me a cautious smile before finishing it.

"Strip," I told him, hurrying out of my jacket and yanking off my top.

"You've really mastered the art of the seductive strip-tease," he grumbled, shrugging out of his jacket.

"Shut up." I rolled my eyes and kicked free of my jeans. Unlike last time, this time I wasn't embarrassed to remove every article of clothing. Grayson had already seen everything, and I was too distracted to care anyway. The water was warm and in addition to masking our conversation, also washed away Elena's blood that had splattered on me.

Grayson filled the empty space behind me in the shower. "Alright, you got me to strip. Care to fill me in now?"

"My hand did something to Logan," I said, whispering

even though no one could hear us while we were under the water.

"Kinky," Grayson replied with a smirk. Sometimes, he just couldn't help himself.

"It burned him," I said, ignoring his comment.

He stared at me. "What do you mean?"

"I can't explain it. I've never experienced anything like it, but when I put my hand on his chest, this charge of energy shot through my hand. It felt like my hand was on fire and Logan could feel it, too. I was burning him from the inside out." I held up my hand, again searching for any sign of that mysterious energy.

"Are you sure?" Grayson said in an oddly calm voice.

I nodded. "Very sure. Why? Does it mean anything to you?"

"Maybe." His head tilted as he looked past me, eyes focused on something much more distant than the tile walls.

When he didn't continue, I poked him in his hard abdominals. "Well?"

"You know about the Founder curse, obviously," Grayson said, absently pushing wet hair away from my face. "If the offspring of a Founder dies before they turn 18, you end up with me, Dorian, and Nick. The part of the curse that is less certain is, what happens to the offspring of a Founder if they don't die?"

"Like me?" I thought for a second. "But the curse isn't supposed to affect the females."

"It's not that it can't affect females, it's just that the female offspring rarely die before the age of 18. For some reason, the males are disproportionately affected by the curse." Grayson ran a hand along the curve of my neck. "What if it isn't just the magic in town that is changing? What if the curse is changing, too?"

It sounded like a stretch, but I didn't have a better explanation. "Even if you are right, that doesn't really explain my new superpower."

"You just turned 18, correct?" he said.

"Yeah, a couple weeks ago. So?"

"So, I owe you a present," he said with a sly grin as his hand moved down my body. "But also, maybe surviving past 18 means you are given a special ability to fight supernatural creatures."

"Why? That doesn't make any sense." I forced myself to ignore Grayson's roaming hand.

Grayson was an excellent multi-tasker. "It's brilliant, really. What better way to punish founding families? The male heirs die and become monsters, the female Hunter heirs live and become super-Hunters. The Founders are destined to be at war with themselves."

"But there are no other female Hunter heirs in the falls," I reminded him. "Just me."

"Now. But that wasn't always the case." He smirked again. "Guess this makes you special, Jones."

"And here I thought I was special all along," I replied.

His hand did an impressive maneuver that made my entire body tense. "You've always been special to me, Isabel."

"We're having a serious conversation," I scolded without much conviction.

"You're naked," he said, his roaming hand only further proving his point as he flicked dots of water from my chest. "And wet."

"Grayson." My face flushed.

He laughed. "So easily embarrassed. I didn't think that would be possible after last night."

"I'm just not as comfortable with the extreme nudity as you and your supernatural friends are," I said pointedly.

"Dorian." Grayson's eyes darkened. "He wanted you to see him."

"He did seem very confident," I said, slowly running my hands over Grayson's chest. I locked my hands behind his neck and tilted my head back. Beads of water dripped from his dark hair and lashes. "Especially considering what he's working with."

Grayson flinched. "You looked?"

"It was hard not to, Grayson." I pushed up on my toes, being careful not to slip. My entire body rubbed against his in a very purposeful way. "Don't worry. You are superior to him in *every* way."

"Damn straight," he replied with a growl, backing me against the tile wall. Any worries about the dangers facing Shaded Falls were washed away by the pounding water and Grayson's kisses. I let myself get lost in him, reveling his touch. It was like he was erasing every bad thought and replacing them with nothing but pleasure.

It wasn't until later, after we had both dried off and dressed in clean clothes and after Grayson had left the bedroom, that my mind wandered back to what he had told me. It was the first I had heard of these potential super-powers. It sounded absurd, and yet it also made some sense. While the energy had fried Logan's vampire heart to ash, it had only warmed my hand. There'd been no pain for me.

When Grayson returned, he caught me staring at my hands. "They are quite impressive," he joked, but I barely heard him.

"He's not going to stop," I said, a sudden realization hitting me like a punch in the gut. "He'll keep killing everyone I love."

"Isabel, what are you talking about?" Grayson's confused

look only angered me. I wasn't telling him anything he didn't already know.

"Liam." I let my hands drop to my sides. "I couldn't save Justin or my father. Steve knew exactly what he was getting himself into, but Elena was innocent. I should have been able to save her."

"How?" Grayson was also getting angry. "You didn't kill Elena, Logan did."

"Because of me," I breathed. "How many more people have to die?"

Grayson stared at me with so much urgency that I felt my eyes fill with unshed tears. "Isabel Jones, listen very carefully to me. Don't even think about turning yourself into Liam. If you do that, you will most certainly be responsible for my death because I can't live without you."

"Don't be so dramatic," I said, blinking away the tears. "You'd be just fine without me. No more human distraction to get in the way of your loyalty to the clan."

"You're still upset about that?" he said through tight lips.

"No. Yes. Honestly, I have no clue why I'm upset." I threw up my hands. "Maybe I had too much whiskey."

He wasn't charmed by my vulnerability this time. "Let me be clear, Isabel. It's you."

"What?" My breathing became very rapid.

"My top priority. The person I'd die for. All that I need to be happy. All of that– it's you." He caught my face in his hands. "It's you now, it's you always. If you don't know that by now, I'm not sure how I'll ever be able to convince you."

"He could kill you, Grayson." Those damn tears were back, threatening to spill over. "I can't let that happen."

Grayson caught a single tear under his thumb and wiped it away. "Don't cry, darling. Nothing is going to happen to me."

I nodded slightly, trying to convince both of us that I believed his words. "I can't lose anyone else," I said, closing my eyes to hold back a flood of tears.

"I know." He kissed my forehead. "I get it, Isabel. Truly. But I need you to promise me right now that you aren't going to sacrifice yourself to save me. No matter what."

"Grayson, I can't promise you that." I opened my eyes. "I wouldn't ask you to make that same promise to me."

He sighed. "I know. But I'm just another vampire, Isabel. I'm not special, like you. Your life matters more than mine."

"You're an idiot," I said coolly.

"Ouch," he said with an exaggerated flinch.

"If you don't know you're special by now, nothing I say is going to convince you," I said, turning his words back on him. I kissed him quickly because I couldn't be this close to him and not kiss him. "Will you do me a favor?"

"Anything."

"Can you drive me to Jim's house? I need to get something." I hoped I sounded nonchalant enough that he wouldn't ask what I needed.

Grayson smiled, relieved that I no longer looked to be on the verge of sobbing. "That sounds easy enough."

"You're an easy mark," I teased. "I was willing to pay you handsomely for the favor."

"I'd be happy to retroactively negotiate payment." The sparkle had returned to his eyes. "But we both know I'm never going to say no to you."

"Sucker." I kissed his cheek. "Thank you. You're the best vampire boyfriend ever."

"Stop, you're making me blush." He turned away from me quickly and I wondered if he actually was blushing. It was impossible to tell with vampires.

Nick was still annoyed that we had borrowed his bike

earlier, so Grayson drove us to Jim's house in his car. It was less exciting than the bike, but I didn't fear for my life the entire time, so that as a plus.

"I think I might prefer vehicles that require you to wrap your body around mine," Grayson said, snaking a hand over to squeeze my thigh.

"No offense, but I prefer vehicles with seatbelts and airbags."

He just laughed and slid his hand higher. "Humans are so risk adverse."

"Silly humans," I said with a grin. Grayson was always at his most adorable when he was feeling playful. "You're such a hero for putting up with me."

"You have a few good traits," he teased. "It's not all misery."

"I don't know. I had you moaning pretty bad earlier." I was facing straight ahead, but from the corner of my eye I saw his head snap in my direction.

"Isabel!" He mocked embarrassment. "Your mind is always in the gutter."

"I wonder where I got that from," I said dryly, giving him a serious look.

He winked and smiled his crooked smile. "I continue to be amazed that I find new things to adore about you."

"Gross." I pretended to gag. "I liked you better when you were just annoyed by me."

"Oh, I'm still annoyed by you." He parked the car and I was surprised to see that we were already at Jim's place. Our banter had been an effective distraction. "You're just very lucky you're a good kisser."

I exited the car without responding. It was weird to approach the abandoned house with only Grayson by my side. Jim's house was a place that I associated with him,

Sadie, and Nick. It was not a part of my life I'd ever expected to invite Grayson into. My mood changed dramatically in the few steps across the yard. Grayson sensed the change instantly and fell into comfortable silence. He read my moods better than anyone and always adapted appropriately.

"Do you think anyone is watching the house?" I asked quietly as I unlocked the door.

"I doubt it." Grayson's eyes darted around. "I'm sure Liam already knows that Jim and Sadie took off and that you've been shacking up with me. He's got no reason to keep eyes on this place."

Out of habit, I locked the door behind us. A locked door wasn't going to stop a vampire, but I wasn't going to make it easy for them if they did happen to attack. I noticed that Grayson was looking toward the kitchen.

"What's wrong? Nick and I cleaned up the blood." I followed his stare.

"I can still smell it," he said quietly.

"Oh. Are you going to be okay?" I remembered how much time Nick and I had spent bleaching the floor and couldn't believe that the scent still lingered. Maybe it was in the air. "I can make this quick."

"I'll be fine." Grayson smiled reassuringly. "Just get what you need. Take your time."

I pointed to the hallway. "It's just in my bedroom."

"Alright." He looked around. "I'll just wait out here."

"Okay." I couldn't seem to make my legs move.

Grayson laughed uncertainly. "Do you need an escort?"

"Do you think we could stay here tonight?" I asked timidly.

"Here?" His eyebrows shot up. "Is my bed not comfortable enough for you?"

I regretted asking. "Never mind."

"Hey." He turned my head with two of his fingers, making me look at him. "Why did you ask me that? Really?"

"Look, I really appreciate you letting me stay at the mansion. I know it's your home and I know it's a big deal that you're letting a Hunter stay there."

"But?" he prodded.

"But there are dozens of vampires always lurking around hearing everything. I just want one night where I don't have to worry about every word I say or... even every noise I make." I gave him a purposeful look.

He nodded, understanding. "I get it. The lack of privacy isn't ideal. Sure, we can stay for one night. Just let me call Trina to tell her I won't be back."

"Trina?" I groaned inwardly. Of course, Grayson had responsibilities at the mansion. I couldn't just ask him to neglect his leadership duties. Other people were depending on him and here I was, whining about a little invasion of privacy. "Forget it, Grayson. You have to go back."

"No, really. They can handle things without me." He already had his phone in hand. "We don't have much to do until the other patrols report back at dawn anyway."

"Are you sure this isn't just your inability to say no to me?" I pushed.

"Eh, maybe." He smirked. "Honestly, I could use a break from all the war planning anyway. A full night of sleep sounds amazing."

Reluctantly, I nodded. "Okay. Call Trina."

It was strange being back in my own bedroom. My bed looked so small compared to Grayson's and when I looked at it, I had a sudden image of being there with Nick. He used to sneak in my window at night and bring me flowers from the meadow. We would curl up in bed and whisper to each other in the dark. For the first time since realizing I was falling for Grayson, I missed Nick.

"This is going to be a challenge," Grayson said when he caught me staring at the bed, misinterpreting my expression. "But I think we can make it work."

"I'm sure we can," I replied, turning away. Nick and I had made it work and Grayson was only an inch or so taller than Nick. "Is Trina handling your absence alright?"

"She couldn't be happier. Trina is always eager for more responsibility." Grayson sat on the edge of the bed. "What are we doing here?"

I walked over to my desk and plucked a book from the shelf above it. "This is Elias Jones' journal. I found it in the special collection at the library."

"A book? We're here because of a book?" Grayson looked disappointed. "I have hundreds of those in my bedroom, Isabel."

"Not this one. It's one of a kind." I took a seat on the desk chair because sitting anywhere near Grayson would not be a good idea. His roaming hands were far too distracting. I flipped open the journal and quickly scanned the old handwriting. "Elias Jones had terrible handwriting. Even worse than yours."

Grayson cleared his throat. "Um, you're familiar with my handwriting?"

"I told you I was going to snoop in your bedroom," I said with a shrug. "I may have found some old love notes you forgot to give to one of your skanky ex-girlfriends."

"Woah. Hold up." Grayson blinked several times. "First, how do you know they were skanky?"

"Really?" I raised an eyebrow. "I mean, obviously they were."

"Second," he proceeded as if I hadn't answered, "what makes you think they are *ex*-girlfriends?"

I shrugged again. "Because you aren't suave enough to juggle multiple girls."

"Third," he continued, plowing right ahead. "You read my private correspondence?"

"Look, I'd love to apologize and say it was an accident and it won't happen again, but we both know that's not true. You can't leave something like that just stuck inside a book on a shelf and then get mad when I read it." I flipped through a few more book pages. "I didn't even know what they were at first."

Grayson's silence was so sudden that I looked up. "Those weren't my letters."

"No?" I was shocked. The words had sound like Grayson, down to the darlings. "Whose were they?"

"My dad wrote them to my mom back when they were dating." He stared at a spot on the floor and twisted his hands together. "I found them after Mom left with Elsie. I'm not sure why she left them behind, but I was glad to have something that reminded me of both my parents."

"He called your mom darling," I said softly.

Grayson nodded and looked up. There was so much pain in his eyes that it took my breath away. Grayson had only told me about his family once, and just that short conversation had torn him apart. I hated that his life had been filled with so much sadness.

"I'm sorry I read them," I said, wishing I could go back in time. It was such a terrible invasion of his family's private history.

"I'm not." He didn't look away as tears filled his eyes. "It's hard for me to talk about them, but I want you to know about them. My dad adored my mother more than anything and his death destroyed her. They were good parents. I know she didn't want to leave me, but she had to keep Elsie safe."

It would be so much easier to hate his mother. She had left him at a time when he needed her the most. But I could also understand why she had done it.

"The letters are beautiful," I said, remembering how I'd been envious when I read them, back when I thought that Grayson had written them for someone that wasn't me. "Your father was quite the romantic."

"It was disgusting," he said with a smile. "They couldn't keep their hands off each other, even after being married for 15 years."

"If your father looked anything like you, I think I can understand." It was hard for me to be sitting even a few feet away from him when every nerve in my body wanted to be touching him.

We exchanged a long look that was full of more meaning than any words either of us could say. I set the book aside and got to my feet. Grayson's gravity was stronger than ever, pulling me across the space between us until he leaned back and opened his arms. I stepped between his legs, rubbing my hands over his shoulders. He stared at me the whole time, eyes never blinking even as I pulled my shirt over my head.

"You're so beautiful," he said, pulling me into his lap. He buried his face in my neck and softly kissed the small scar Nick had left when he fed on me. It was strange to think about Grayson's lips pressing over the exact spot where Nick's lips had been, albeit under very different circumstances.

"Is it hard for you to hold back with me?" I whispered.

Grayson lifted his head. "No. Not a single part of me would ever consider doing something that would hurt you,

Isabel."

I ran my hand over the back of his head, burying my fingers in his dark waves. "I don't just mean the thirst, Grayson. I have to imagine that our physical contact would be much different if I had vampire strength."

"I like being gentle with you, darling." His hands softly skimmed down my spine. "It's nice to have one thing in my life that isn't defined by being a vampire. It's nice to feel human again."

"If you had the choice to be human, would you take it?" I hated that I didn't already know what his answer would be. I was still getting to know basic, crucial things about Grayson.

"In a second," he said. "I can't think of anything better than growing old with you."

I groaned inwardly. He was too perfect to be real. "You know, you've already got me topless in your lap. The flattery is just overkill at this point."

He laughed and kissed my shoulder. "What about you? Would you ever think about becoming a vampire?"

"Become a vampire?" I pulled away slightly with a stunned look.

"You've never even considered it?" he said, surprised that I was so surprised.

"No." I shook my head furiously. "Why would I consider that?"

A flash of hurt flooded his eyes. "Maybe because you're in love with a vampire?"

"I am," I said quickly. "But that doesn't mean that I want to join you in the blood sucking, Grayson."

"It doesn't have to be all bad," he said, his arms a little stiffer around me. "You don't have to kill people. I've never killed anyone."

"You almost killed Elsie," I reminded him softly, running

my hand over his neck. I knew that my words were hurting him, but I had to be honest. I had never once thought about becoming a vampire.

"If you don't become a vampire and I don't find some miraculous way to become human, our relationship has an expiration date." He smiled sadly. "Guess we'll just have to make the most of the time we have."

I giggled as he flipped me onto the bed. He lay next to me and I rolled onto my side to face him. "Are you mad that I said no?"

"Never. Your humanity is a big part of why I love you so much." He rested a hand on my hip.

"I thought it was my body," I teased.

"This body?" He ran his hand up my side to my chest. "I'm not complaining."

"What happened to all that flattery you were throwing around earlier?" My heart was thumping hard beneath his hand. Grayson ignored me, his lips already busy making my skin hum with pleasure.

We struggled talking about personal things, but this was something we did well. There was no hesitation or guessing when it came to our physical intimacy. We were both perfectly content to say with our bodies what we couldn't say with words.

7

A fterward, Grayson fell asleep almost immediately and I had to marvel at how quickly he shifted from sexual master to sleeping beauty. He had kept his arms around me, but I slipped away without waking him. I pulled on Grayson's shirt and grabbed the journal before slinking away to the kitchen where I could read with a light on. After heating up water for tea, I hunched over the book at the kitchen table, starting at the very beginning.

Elias had done a lot of research into the magical spells that had cursed the founding families and enchanted the falls. Even after he turned 18, when it was no longer a risk that he would be forced to transition, he had feverishly researched a way to reverse the curse. What was more interesting to me was Elias' older sister, Annie. She was just one year older than Elias and had also made it into adulthood without dying.

If Grayson was right about my new power being tied to my founding family heritage, Annie could hold the answers I needed. The only problem was that Elias was quite self-centered and hardly mentioned his sister. Yet he had no problem filling pages with strange doodles and passages of words written in an ancient language.

"Hey, you coming back to bed anytime soon? I'm lonely."

Grayson's voice startled me. I had been so busy trying to decipher the text that I hadn't noticed him staring at me from the doorway.

"You are far too comfortable with your body," I said, noting his absence of clothing.

"In my defense, someone stole my shirt," he said with a dazzling grin. His voice was still thick with sleep and his hair was a disaster.

"It's a good thing you are drop-dead gorgeous," I said with a sigh. "Otherwise, I'd never be able to put up with you."

He winked. "Come to bed, Jones. Keep me warm."

"Might as well. There's nothing useful in this journal anyway." I slapped it closed and followed Grayson down the hall.

"What exactly are you hoping to find?"

"Elias had a sister, Annie, that lived past 18. I thought maybe he would mention if she possessed any weird powers." I threw the book on my desk and dove onto the bed, thoroughly defeated. "Nothing."

Grayson eased himself next to me and I curled around him. "Why don't you just read Annie's journal?"

"Good idea, Einstein," I grumbled. "Obviously, I don't have Annie's journal."

"No, you don't. But I do." He cocked a triumphant smile when I raised my head to stare at him.

"You do? How?" I poked him in the ribs. "Why are you waiting until now to tell me?"

"I had no idea what you were trying to find. You never even told me what you needed to get from Jim's house until we got here." He tugged playfully on a strand of my hair. "You need to learn to use your words, Jones."

I poked him again. "No more talking. I'm mad at you."

He just laughed and closed his eyes. "Get some rest, darling. You've got school in the morning."

School. How absurd. It seemed like a lifetime had passed since I had last been there, but it had only been a few hours. So much had happened since then. Elena was dead. I'd killed Logan with just my touch. The last thing I wanted to do was sit through hours of pointless classes, but part of my deal with Jim was that I wouldn't drop out of school while he was gone. One thing I refused to do was break a promise to Jim.

I wasn't surprised that I had a nightmare about Elena's death. I was sure I would be traumatized by the sight of her bleeding out on the cabin floor for a long time. I was surprised when Grayson shook me awake and my cheeks were wet with tears. He simply wiped them away with his hands and folded me into a tight embrace. I knew that he wouldn't mention it in the morning. My grief wasn't something he would force me to dissect and analyze. Somehow, Grayson always new exactly how to handle me.

Morning came far too soon and it was strange getting ready for school in my old bedroom. In such a short amount of time, I'd gotten use to life in the mansion. Grayson put on his clothes from the day before, complaining with a smile that his shirt now smelled like me. I made it up to him with a long kiss that turned into much more and made me late for homeroom.

The first half of the day passed normally. One class turned into another turned into another until it was time for lunch and then that too had passed. I thought I was going to make it through the whole school day without having to face the reality of Elena's death. As long as I kept busy taking notes and solving math problems, I could keep the image of Elena's dead body from rising too close to the surface.

It was only after lunch that I noticed the shift in the atmosphere. It started when I stopped to use the restroom and found three girls crying at the sink. I didn't know any of them well enough to ask why they were crying, but I suspected it wasn't the result of a breakup or failed test.

In the next period, a burst of static broke over the intercom and my suspicions were confirmed. The principal asked all seniors to head to the school gym for an urgent assembly. I followed the throng of oblivious students, dreading what was about to happen. It wasn't just Elena that had died last night. Three other girls had also been murdered by Logan. This assembly was about to devastate the student body and I was the only one that knew the truth about how their friends had died.

I noticed a row of school staff members sitting on the front row of the bleachers. Dorian was with them, though sitting a few feet away from the baseball coach. With no other friends left in school, I strolled over and sat directly behind him.

"Gotta say, I didn't see this coming," he said without turning to look at me.

"What have you heard about Liam?" I asked. Grayson had been ignoring my texts all day, either because he was busy or because he thought I should be busy doing things other than texting him. I was anxious to hear if anyone had learned anything helpful during the patrols.

"Gray keeping you in the dark?" Dorian shot a glance over his shoulder, obvious humor in his eyes. "Careful with that one. He keeps a lot of secrets."

"Maybe he just keeps them from you because you screwed his girlfriend," I snapped.

Dorian chuckled. "It takes two to tango, Jones. Kate was a willing participant. Maybe if Gray had satisfied her better, she wouldn't have crawled eagerly into my bed."

"It's refreshing to know you've always been an asshole and it's not just an unfortunate were trait." My hands balled into fists and I regretted my decision to sit by him. Why had I thought that Dorian Anderson would provide a single shred of comfort or support?

The principal kicked off the assembly, breaking the news to everyone that four of our classmates had been viciously murdered. The gym dissolved into a chorus of wails and tears. Dorian looked around with casual annoyance.

"Why are you even here?" I asked when I caught him rolling his eyes and sighing.

"Because I knew you would be here." He gave me another glance that was surprising. If I didn't know better, I'd say I detected some sympathy in his eyes. "One of the girls was your friend, right?"

"Yes," I said.

"I'm sorry." He half-turned in his seat, putting a hand on my knee. "I want Liam dead as much as you and Gray. I know you think I'm a monster, and you have good reason to think that, but I'm not like Liam. I don't believe in slaughtering innocent humans."

I nodded as I processed his words and was surprised that we had found a common ground. I was also surprised that his touch wasn't completely repulsive. "If Grayson finds out you touched my knee, he'll rip out your heart."

"He can try," Dorian said with a grimace, but he removed his hand.

The rest of the school day was canceled, in addition to

the rest of the week. Students were encouraged to stay after the assembly to speak with grief counselors, but I was in a hurry to leave. It was only when I was almost out the door that I noticed her – Sloan. She was standing with a group of girls from our class and she was crying.

"Isabel!" She waved me over with one hand while using her other hand to wipe tears from her cheeks.

After a few seconds of shock, I slowly approached her. The last time I saw Sloan, she'd been compelled to use her magical abilities to attack Grayson's clan. I'd had to physically slam into her, knocking her unconscious, to break the spell.

"Hey, Sloan." I desperately searched her eyes to see if she was compelled right at that moment.

"I've been looking everywhere for you," she whispered, grabbing my arm as her eyes darted around. "We need to talk. Someplace private."

"I, uh, I'm in a hurry," I said, glancing at the door.

Sloan leaned closer. "I'm not compelled anymore," she whispered.

My breath caught in my throat. It could be a trick. Maybe Liam had compelled her to lie about being compelled, but I didn't think so. There was too much desperation in her eyes. Against my better judgment, I said, "Okay, but someone is waiting on me. Will you come with me?"

"Yes." She nodded enthusiastically.

Since Grayson had driven me to school, Sloan had to play chauffeur. I told her we were going to the mansion and she stared at me blankly. At first, I thought it was just a nervous reaction to returning to a place filled with vampires she had tortured, but then she asked for directions.

"You remember the mansion, right? You were there

Saturday night." It hadn't occurred to me that she might not remember some of what happened that night.

"I don't remember anything from Saturday night," she said, gripping the steering while tighter. "I was under compulsion when they cornered me at the dance."

"How did you break the compulsion?" I said.

Her head shook. "I don't know. It just happened last night. I was in this weird hypnotic state for the last couple of days and then suddenly," she snapped two of her fingers, "the haze was gone and I was me again."

"Turn right here," I said, pointing. "You'll see the mansion on the left."

"Whoa. It really is a mansion." Sloan smiled, looking more like herself. "This is where you are living now?"

"Temporarily," I said. "This is Grayson's place."

Her eyes widened. "Grayson? That 'friend' who picked you up from school?"

"We're a little more than friends," I admitted as she parked. "But more importantly, it's a lair for vampires, so let me go first and do the talking, okay?"

"Gladly." She smirked at me. "But I'm going to need more details on the Grayson situation later."

"I'll pencil in time for us to talk," I said with a laugh. It was good to have Sloan back, even if I didn't know how it had happened. As we walked toward the house, I cautioned her, "Last time you were here, you kind of tried to help Liam kill everyone. Just FYI."

"I what?" Her eyes widened in horror and she stopped mid-step.

I looped my arm through hers, dragging her forward. "It'll be fine. Grayson won't let anyone hurt you."

"Because he trusts you?" she said.

"Because he's a good man." For the first time ever, I let

myself into the mansion. If I wanted Sloan to feel comfortable there, she needed to see me looking comfortable there. I also wanted to catch the vampires by surprise. The less time they had to react to Sloan's arrival, the better my chance of getting to Grayson first.

"Grayson," I called out softly from the entryway. Presumably, he was somewhere deep in the house meeting with Trina and the council. Unless he was on our balcony, he would hear me calling his name and would eventually come to me.

"In here!"

I hadn't expected to hear a response from the room closest to where we stood. Sloan actually jumped slightly.

"It'll be okay," I whispered. "Stay behind me."

Grayson would've heard that, too, and I was sure he was already bracing himself for our appearance in the room. When I rounded the corner with Sloan close behind, a half-dozen vampires all stood waiting for us. Grayson was the only one that didn't look like he was about to lunge at us.

"Look who I found," I said with a forced smile.

"Explain quickly, Isabel." Grayson wasn't in a playful mood.

"Her compulsion has been broken," I said, skipping right to the information he would care about most.

"Isabel, I know you want that to be true, but unless Liam is dead it's not possible. She's lying to you." Grayson's hand twitched at his side, the only sign that he was as anxious as the other vamps.

Sloan spoke only to me. "Liam isn't the one who compelled me."

"What?" I stared at her. "If Liam didn't, who did?"

"It was Elena's brother, Logan. He's a vampire, too." Sloan noticed the look I exchanged with Grayson. "What?"

"Logan was killed last night," I explained, leaving out the part about how he had died. "That's why your compulsion broke."

Grayson took a step forward. "So, she's really free of compulsion? That's good news for us."

"Thought you might like it." I smiled smugly and he parried with a smile that made my heart flutter.

"If you weren't already my favorite human, this would do the trick," he said.

"Aw." Sloan elbowed me in the side. "You two are adorable."

I flushed and Grayson cleared his throat. "Sloan, I have a few questions I'd like to ask if you are willing to sit down with me for a bit."

"Hold up, Parker," I said, holding out a hand. "Before you ask her anything, I'd like to make a deal."

"A deal?" A glimmer of a smirk pulled up one corner of his lips. His eyes sparkled with humor. "Proceed."

"Sloan needs a place to stay. Liam is obviously going to want to compel her again. If she answers your questions and tells you everything she knows about his clan and their plans, I want you to let her stay in the mansion and guarantee her safety." I didn't so much as blink as I made my demands.

Grayson had already made a big statement when he offered me his protection. Making a deal with the weres had only added to his list of unusual vampire overlord behaviors. If there were still members of his clan skeptical of his leadership abilities, protecting a powerful witch wasn't likely to persuade them.

His jaw was clenched tightly as he appraised me. The humor in his eyes was gone, replaced with unguarded distrust. I knew that he had a very difficult time saying no to me and I hoped that would extend to protecting Sloan as well. Logically, Grayson didn't have much choice. If he sent Sloan away, it would only be a matter of time before she was under Liam's thrall. But if I was wrong to trust her and she was still compelled, Grayson would be planting a Trojan horse right in the heart of his clan.

"We have a deal," he said. "But only if she helps us."

"I will," Sloan said eagerly. "I'll tell you everything I know."

Grayson turned to the vampires behind him. "Tell the others. The witch is to be protected as long as she is under this roof."

There were reluctant head nods and angry glances in our direction, but they relaxed from their battle stances. I checked to see how Sloan was holding up and she looked remarkably more relaxed than Grayson.

"Welcome to the family," I said glibly.

Grayson brushed past me, his arm grazing mine only accidentally. It made my skin tingle nonetheless. "We need to do this right now, Sloan."

"Oh, okay." She looked to me for confirmation. "Where should we do this?"

"Follow me," Grayson said gruffly, stepping past her and into the hallway. I took a step forward and he turned to stop me. "Stay here."

"Excuse you?" I said.

"I will handle this alone, Isabel," he said in his overlord voice.

Every part of me wanted to argue with him. He knew better than to use that voice with me. But I'd already challenged him in a big way by demanding sanctuary for Sloan. He still needed to have some semblance of authority if the other vampires were going to follow his orders, so I backed down.

"Okay." I nodded and told Sloan, "Go with Grayson. You'll be fine."

She wasn't convinced, but she followed him anyway.

8

Nick came into the room shortly after Grayson disappeared with Sloan and he waved a hand for me to follow him. He didn't want Grayson to know he was talking to me. That was odd behavior, even for Nick. I was intrigued enough to go along with his game, following him through the mansion and into the backyard.

"This should be far enough," Nick said, stopping at the edge of a garden that hadn't seen an actual flower in probably a decade. "We should be far enough away that Gray won't be able to eavesdrop."

"Why would he even want to?" I said. "He's not jealous of you, Nick. He doesn't care if we talk."

"He's not jealous *anymore*. He won," Nick said, not unkindly.

"Can we just skip to whatever you wanted to tell me?" A conversation with Nick about Grayson was never going to end well.

"I think I might know someone that can help us fight Liam," Nick said. "He's a Hunter who also happens to be married to a witch."

"A Hunter? That's not possible. I'm the only Hunter in the falls," I said.

Nick's eyes darted up in a quick motion that was painfully familiar to me. He was annoyed. "No kidding, Iz. This Hunter doesn't live in the falls, obviously."

"Then how do you know him?" I was growing annoyed, too, and was also wondering how in the world the two of us had ever dated without killing each other. "You weren't even able to leave the falls for the three years you were undead, Nick. Excuse me for finding it hard to believe that you made friends with someone outside of town."

"His name is David." Nick paused. His face twisted briefly as he forced himself to continue. "David Rockson. My uncle, Dave."

"Your uncle?" I punched him hard in the arm. "You have an uncle who is a Hunter and you never thought to mention it?"

Nick shrugged. "It didn't seem relevant."

"Not relevant?" I thought about hitting his arm again, but I was afraid I might accidentally miss on purpose and hit him in the face. "Forget the Hunter part and let's start with you never mentioning that you have an uncle."

"Why would that come up?" he asked, closing in on my incredulousness.

"We talked about our families when we were dating, Nick." I took a deep breath. "You told me Sadie raised you alone, that you didn't have any other family."

He shook his head. "That's not what I said. I said my mom didn't have any family to help raise me, and she didn't. Uncle Dave was never around. He moved away when my dad died and he never came back to the falls."

"He doesn't sound like the kind of guy that will want to help us," I said.

"Then I'll make him." Nick glared off into the distance. "Your boyfriend is looking for you."

I glanced back at the mansion just as Sloan bounded outside. She looked far more relaxed after her chat with Grayson, but she was surprised to see me with Nick.

"Sorry to interrupt." She smiled hesitantly.

"You're not interrupting," I assured her.

"Rockson." Grayson stood at the door. He looked only at Nick, while Sloan stared at me. "Come with me."

Nick rolled his eyes at me. "I don't know what you see in that guy," he muttered.

"Funny, he says the same thing about you," I said with a smirk.

With one last annoyed glare, Nick followed Grayson inside. Sloan opened her mouth the second they were gone. "Okay, I *have* to know what happened there. How did you break up with Nick and then immediately score a hot vampire boyfriend?"

"It wasn't immediate," I said, wondering if they were both truly out of earshot. "Let's walk out there." I pointed toward the far side of the yard where there was a concrete bench. "This is going to be a long conversation and you'll probably want to be seated."

She nodded and followed me through the overgrown grass. "Are you really dating Grayson?" she said.

"Yes, I am."

"You don't care that he's a vampire?"

I dropped onto the bench with a sigh. "It wouldn't have been my first choice, but you don't really get to choose who you fall in love with."

"Love?" She looked startled as she sat next to me. "I had just assumed you were in it for the hot vampire sex."

I laughed. "If only it were that simple."

"Alright, start at the beginning." Sloan folded her legs under her and looked at me expectantly. "I want all the sexy details."

I hadn't planned to tell her every detail but once I started talking, it all spilled out. Nick being undead when I met him. Dorian trying to pit us against each other and Nick choosing to become a vampire by feeding off me. Grayson becoming our ally. Nick breaking up with me. Grayson declaring his love for me. Me falling for Grayson. The battle against Liam. Killing Logan after watching him kill Elena.

This last part was the hardest part to tell her. Sloan had known Elena since they were just young girls. They were practically sisters.

"I'm so sorry, Sloan. I failed her." I looked hard at the dirt and blinked back tears. "I'm sorry about what happened to you, too. I should've found a way to protect you."

"I'm a powerful witch and I couldn't even protect myself," she said through her tears. "None of this is your fault. Liam is evil."

"What did you tell Grayson?" I asked.

"As much as I could remember." She used the sleeve of her shirt to wipe the tears from her cheeks. "I was kept in a room by myself. I don't remember much from when I was under the compulsion. Last night, I felt an icy chill run through my body and I was me again. I could think clearly and was in complete control of my actions. I could use my magic as I wanted to use it, not how I was compelled to use it. That's how I was able to escape."

I had so many questions I wanted to ask her, but I didn't want to overwhelm Sloan. She had gone through a lot over the last few days and had also faced a Grayson interrogation. Right now, she just needed a friend.

"Grayson wasn't too tough, was he?" I asked. "He means

well, but sometimes he forgets to turn off his carefully curated superior attitude."

"Grayson?" She giggled. "He was really sweet, actually. I get why you fell for him."

"Grayson was sweet?" It was my turn to be surprised. "That must've been hard for him."

"He isn't sweet with you?" She wasn't judging, just being a concerned friend.

It only took a second for me to smile. "No, he is. He just has a hard time showing that side of him to anyone else."

"He's a guy, Izzy. Guys aren't always great with the whole feelings thing." She waved a hand in the air. "As long as he's good to you and isn't off killing humans, you should just enjoy being in love."

"I can't believe you and I are having a conversation right now about my vampire boyfriend," I said with a disbelieving shake of my head.

"It does feel like we should both be drunk right now to be talking about something like this," she said with a laugh.

I jumped to my feet. "I can make that happen."

"Really?" She looked doubtful.

"My boyfriend is 23-years-old. There's plenty of booze in the mansion." I grabbed her hand and pulled her up. "Let's go."

"You're sure this is a good idea? Aren't you at war with Liam?" She was protesting in words only, her hurried steps matched mine easily.

I slowed just a little. "Should we be worried about him attacking us tonight?"

"I doubt it. He's not staying in the falls. We were in a town about thirty minutes away. By now, he has to know that I've come here and he'll be too afraid to attack right away. I could easily use my powers on him." She grinned. "And will be very happy to do that."

"We have some time then?" I said.

"I think so. He'll need time to come up with a plan for how to overpower me." She pushed her shoulders back proudly.

We were inside now and I headed straight to the kitchen. A couple of vampires were milling around with their blood beverages, but I ignored them and headed straight to the bar.

"Tomorrow, we worry about Liam." I grabbed a bottle of whiskey. "Tonight, we drink!"

We were three drinks in, sitting on the kitchen floor, when Grayson found us.

"Parker! Come have a drink with us," I said a little too loudly, waving the whiskey bottle at him. The other vampires in the room all watched the exchange with obvious smirks.

He eyed me curiously. "Are you drunk?"

"Little bit," I admitted with a smile. "Is that an issue?"

"No." His smile was faint but genuine. "You really shouldn't sit on the floor though. I have no idea when that was last cleaned and these vampires live like animals."

"Fine. I will get up if you promise to get drunk with us." I gave him a mischievous smile and held out my hand. "Do we have a deal, Parker?"

His lips turned up in a sexy smile and he snatched my hand and pulled me to my feet in one fluid move. While still holding onto me, he took the whiskey bottle with his free hand and took a long drink from it. "We have a deal, Jones," he said.

Sloan let out a happy yelp and climbed to her feet on her

second try. With wide eyes and big smile, she said, "We should have a party!"

Grayson's smile faltered. "A party?"

I had to duck my head to hide my grin. Grayson was not a social person and he hated parties. He had invited me to the last party they'd had at the mansion and we'd spent the entire night alone on the third-floor balcony.

"It'll be fun!' Sloan declared confidently.

Her smile was dazzling and she was working her beauty hard as she fluttered her eyelashes at him. Sloan wasn't flirting, this was just what she did to get her way. She knew the effect that a beautiful woman could have on a man.

"Fun?" Grayson looked unmoved by her charms. His eyes darted to me for support.

"It's a party, Grayson," I said with a shrug. "What could it hurt?"

He groaned and took another drink from the whiskey bottle. "Fine. Do whatever you want."

Sloan clapped her hands and did a little dance that made several of the male vampires leer in her direction. While they were looking at her, I took the opportunity to lean closer to Grayson, kissing his cheek. "Thank you," I said.

"You're going to be the death of me, Isabel Jones," he said with a crooked smile that shattered my heart into a million pieces. "But what a wonderful death it will be."

"Careful, Parker. I've had just enough to drink that I might jump your bones right here in the kitchen," I said, not even caring that everyone could hear me.

For maybe the first time ever, Grayson didn't look around to see who was listening and watching. He hooked a finger into the waistband of my jeans and pulled me close to him. "Don't make a threat like that if you don't intend to follow through."

"Please, don't follow through," Nick said as he walked into the room. He didn't look in our direction, but he didn't look mad. Grayson let out a sudden laugh and I wondered just how much whiskey he'd been drinking. It took a lot of booze to get a vampire drunk.

"She can't anyway," Sloan said, unapologetically pulling me away from Grayson. "We've got a party to plan."

Regret returned to Grayson's eyes the second we were no longer touching. Before he could take back his approval, I said, "I won't let her go too crazy."

He nodded once. "Good."

Sloan looped her arm through mine and pulled me away. "Don't worry, loverboy. I won't keep her too long. She'll still be all hot and bothered when I bring her back to you."

Grayson flinched at her casual tease and I laughed at his stunned expression. I was really enjoying seeing the two opposites interact. Maybe Sloan could shake Grayson from his stuffy shell.

Sloan moved around the mansion, waving her hands and muttering incantations. The effect was truly magical – ornate chandeliers casting ethereal light into normally darkened rooms and music playing from hidden speakers. One of the vampires had taken the initiative to make a booze run and returned with more alcohol than we could drink in a year.

The weres arrived after dark, expecting to be talking battle strategy. After a quick update from Grayson, they easily settled into the party atmosphere. I would've liked to enjoy the festive atmosphere, but Sloan had other plans.

"You can't wear *that*," she said, waving at my clothes, "to a party."

"I don't have any party clothes here, Sloan." I tugged at the hem of my sweater. "This will have to do."

Trina strolled up to us. "I can help you with that. Come."

Of all the vampires, Trina had been the hardest for me to decipher. She was usually cool and aloof, not too dissimilar from Grayson. But she also had lent me her clothes on more than one occasion and had followed orders from me without question when we were battling Liam. She didn't hate me, but I wasn't sure that she liked me.

Sloan was unaware of any awkwardness and happily sailed upstairs after Trina. I had never been in any of the other vampires' rooms and I wasn't sure what to expect. Trina's room was surprisingly normal– bed with floral comforter, dresser littered with hair products and jewelry, overflowing closet bursting with clothes and shoes.

I sat on the edge of the bed as Sloan and Trina happily assembled their wardrobes. In a matter of minutes, Sloan had managed to befriend Trina in a way that I would never be able to do. It was a gift almost as impressive as her magical abilities.

"We'll have to pick something out for her," Sloan told Trina, gesturing to me. "She's a reluctant participant in this party."

Trina grabbed a sparkling black dress and tossed it at me. "Put that on, Hunter."

I was still a little buzzed from the whiskey and feeling excited to have one night that wouldn't be about fighting and death, so I put the dress on without protest. When Trina slapped four-inch heels into my hand, I frowned before putting them on. This outfit wasn't exactly me, but a look in her full-length mirror disagreed.

The dress was a satiny black material that hugged the curves of my body perfectly. The top was fairly conservative, with long sleeves and just a hint of cleavage. The bottom was a different story. The fabric barely reached the top of my thighs.

"Your legs are killer in that dress," Sloan declared as she put the finishing touches on her own outfit.

"Just ask Grayson to be gentle with that zipper later," Trina said.

It was a comment that would've made me blush if anyone else had been in the room, but Trina wasn't saying it to embarrass me. Sloan flipped her hair over her shoulder and grinned. "Alright, we all look fabulous. Let's go get our party on!"

She and Trina left the room arm-in-arm and I felt a pang of sadness as I thought about Elena. I followed a few steps behind them, pausing at the top of the winding staircase to observe the party below. It was strange to see vampires and weres mingling so comfortably under one roof.

I spotted Grayson, leaning casually against the wall with his hands shoved into his pockets. He was wearing a midnight blue sweater with the sleeves pushed up to his elbows and I could see the defined muscles of his body even through the soft cotton fabric. Dark blue jeans hung perfectly on his hips. He really was the most perfect male I had ever seen and I smiled as I studied him from a distance. Two vampires stood before him, talking about something that barely held his attention.

I couldn't stand looking at him without being able to see his face. I hungered for his eyes to look into mine and uttered his name in an imploring whisper, "Grayson."

9

Grayson's beautiful gold eyes flew to me immediately and he straightened, pushing away from the wall in a smooth motion. I took my time on the stairs, still adjusting to the sharp stilettos under my heels. I was aware that Grayson wasn't the only one watching me, but my eyes were locked only onto him. At the bottom of the stairs, he held out his hand.

"Flawless," he said with an awed shake of his head. "Inside and out."

I put my hand in his, sliding my fingers softly over his palm. "I was just thinking the same thing."

Hand-holding was the most physical contact we ever engaged in while in the presence of the vampires. I wanted to respect Grayson's desire to appear in control in front of them and I deferred to his lead whenever gold eyes were watching us. Tonight, Grayson didn't seem to notice any eyes other than mine. He pulled me close and kissed me softly on the lips.

"What are you doing?" I whispered with wide eyes.

"I'm kissing my beautiful girlfriend," he said before

kissing me again, harder and longer this time. He moved his lips to my ear and said, "You look sexy as hell in that dress. I can't wait to take it off you later."

I gasped, mortified, and buried my face into the crook of his neck. With Trina's heels, I was nearly as tall Grayson. "What has gotten into you?" I said, words muffled with my lips pressed to his skin.

"Sloan said the party is supposed to be fun. I have fun flirting with you." He ran his hand along my side, from my hip to the side of my breast. "I have fun touching you."

"In that case, after you take this dress off me later, you can touch me wherever you want, for as long as you want," I said with my lips brushing over his neck.

"Izzy!" Sloan was yelling my name from somewhere in the mansion. With a very great effort, I pulled my head away from Grayson and he groaned.

"I thought she was done with you," he grumbled as I gently removed his hand from my body, instead interlocking our fingers together. I was surprised to see that we were alone in the room now.

"Oh, good. There you are." Sloan handed me a glass. "I brought you a drink."

"What's in this?" I said, giving it is a hesitant sniff. The strong smell of alcohol made me flinch. "Is this gasoline?"

Sloan grinned. "It's a Sloan Special. You'll love it. Just enough alcohol that even *you* will let loose and have fun tonight." She winked at Grayson. "You can thank me later."

She floated away from us, smiling happily. Grayson had already freed his hand from my grip and moved it back to my hip. I took a small sip from the glass and nearly gagged. "I think the Sloan Special is poison."

"It can't be that bad," Grayson said doubtfully. He took it from me, sniffed it with a wrinkle of his nose and then sipped. "No, you're right. That's poison. Better drink it fast."

"Don't worry, lover." I put my hand on the back of his neck and pulled his face to mine. "You're getting laid tonight no matter what."

Our third kiss was far more passionate than the first two. Grayson backed me up against the wall and my leg curled around his body. His hand skimmed over my thigh as he kissed me until I nearly fainted from lack of oxygen.

"Get a room," Dorian said as he came into the room, followed by three female weres. They appeared to be jostling for position next to him.

"This *is* my room," Grayson said coldly. "You're a guest in my house, remember?"

"She's a pretty girl, Parker. You should try taking her out to a nice dinner instead of publicly shagging her at a super-natural rager." Dorian flopped onto a couch and the girls nearly knocked each other over as they fought for the seats on either side of him.

I glared at Dorian and waited for Grayson to rebuke him with harsh reply, but that didn't happen. Instead, Grayson slowly extricated himself from my embrace. "Come," he said, taking my hand and tugging me toward the door.

"She's your girlfriend, not a piece of cattle, Parker," Dorian called after us.

Grayson's grip on my hand tightened and he muttered something under his breath. Fun and flirty Grayson was gone in an instant. He kept walking through the crowd, his angry eyes searching for someplace to go where we wouldn't be swarmed by partygoers.

"Don't let him do this," I said, yanking him to a stop in the middle of a room. "Dorian is scum and he's just being a jerk."

"He's not wrong," Grayson said, finally looking at me. "Do you realize I've never even taken you on a date? We just train and fight and spend all our free time locked away in this mansion."

"That's not all we do," I said, putting a hand on his chest. "We also have lots of really great sex."

His eyes darkened. "Don't. This isn't a joke, Isabel."

"Well, it isn't serious either, Grayson. I don't care about dates and flowers or anything else teenage girls want from teenage boys." I gave him my firmest look. "I just want you."

"I bet you cared about those things when you were dating Rockson," he said, still frowning. "I didn't even take you to that damn dance."

"There will be other dances," I said, putting a second hand on his chest. "I'll dance with you anytime you want, sweetheart. All you have to do is ask."

At that, he smiled. "Sweetheart?"

"Just something I'm trying out," I said with a smirk. "Would you prefer sweetcheeks?"

"You can call me anything you want, darling," he said, the sparkle finally returning to his eyes. He brushed my hair over my shoulder and let his hand linger on the side of my neck. "How long do we need to stay at this party?"

"It's only been, like, 15 minutes," I said with a giggle. "You really don't like having fun, do you?"

"This isn't my idea of fun." He moved his fingers slowly down to my collarbone. "My idea of fun requires us to be alone."

I closed my eyes and sighed. Deep down, all I wanted was to be alone with Grayson. I loved our quiet conversations and the way he looked at me like there was nothing else in the world that mattered to him. I loved how he would say things that would make me laugh and blush and feel beautiful and strong all at the same time. I loved how he let down his guard with me and told me things that no one else knew. I loved how I did the same thing with him. We were so good together that there didn't seem to be any reason to bring anyone else into our world. Except we had to do that very thing because we couldn't possibly beat Liam on our own.

"We have all night to be alone," I said, pulling away. "Let's stay just a little while longer, okay? I think it's important for them to see you here."

"Why?" He gaped at me, dumbfounded.

"Because this isn't just about your clan anymore, Grayson. The weres are here, too, and Sloan. They don't trust you. They don't know you. But you need them to be loyal to you. If you let them see you the way I see you, they will start to trust you." I gave him an imploring look. "We need them on our side. We can't win without them."

He nodded, stroking my hair. "You're right. As always."

"Damn straight." I kissed him one last time and then shoved him away. "Go make friends. Try talking about the weather or sports or something."

"I know how to talk to people, Isabel," he grumbled, pouting like a child.

"Sure you do." I smiled patronizingly. "One hour. Give it one hour and then I'm all yours."

He raised his hand to his temple in a mock salute. "Yes, ma'am."

"Don't ever call me that again," I said with a grimace before turning away, searching the room for Sloan. I found her in the room with the loudest music, chatting happily with a group of weres. I should've known better than to worry about whether she was fitting in. Everyone loved

Sloan, even weres and vamps. I wish I had just a fraction of her charm.

"Izzy!" She waved frantically. "We're playing this really fun game. You have to play with us."

I perched on the couch next to her and took the beer she handed me. "What's the game? Drink until you throw up?"

"That's not the official name," one of the male weres said with a smirk that flashed a dimple. I was pretty sure his name was Jeremy. "But you're also not wrong."

"Alright, I'm in." If I was going to commit for an hour, I might as well have something to do besides dodge Dorian and Nick.

The game was pretty simple. It involved trying to get higher cards than the other people playing the game. Unfortunately, I was not good at the game and Sloan was even worse. She lost so frequently that I wondered if she was doing it on purpose. The more she had to drink, the more she flirted with Jeremy.

"He's so cute," she whispered loudly to me.

"You're so drunk," I replied.

"Only just a bittle lit," she said and her face scrunched. "Little bit."

I laughed. "How about I get you some water?"

"I wike water. Like water." She giggled. "I'm drunk."

"Stay here, Sloany. I'll be right back." I turned to Jeremy. "Don't let her drink anymore, okay?"

He nodded. "I'll keep an eye on her."

I navigated my way past very drunk supernaturals and made it to the kitchen after only one wrong turn. Before I could even think about getting Sloan's water, I stopped dead in my tracks. Grayson was doing what I'd asked him to do, chatting with one of the partygoers, but it wasn't someone I had ever wanted to see him with. I especially didn't want to see him letting this person put her hand on his chest.

Katelyn.

He saw me glaring in their direction and froze in mid-sentence. Katelyn spun to see what had caused his paralysis and narrowed her eyes at me. The last time I saw Katelyn was when she helped Dorian abduct, torture, and turn Nick.

"Isabel Jones," she said with a sneer. "I see you're still a human."

"I see you're still making moves on my boyfriends," I said. "Have you ever thought about not being completely horrible?"

"I don't want your boyfriend, Isabel," she said, flipping her hair. "I've already had him. Actually, I had both your boyfriends first. Apparently, you just love my sloppy seconds."

Grayson tensed. "Kate, stop."

"Oh, get over yourself, Gray. I'm not here to hook up with you and I'm not here to fight with her." Katelyn rolled her pretty eyes.

"Why are you here?" I said through gritted teeth. "This party is for weres and vamps, not evil beasts."

"Isabel," Grayson said with a cautioning look. "Dorian invited her."

I glared at him. "This is your house, Grayson. You can uninvite her."

"We're not exactly in a position to turn away allies," he said firmly. Grayson's famous stoicism had returned as he stepped past Katelyn. "Kate, you can stay as long as you leave Isabel alone and don't ever touch me again."

"You're a shitty host, Gray," Katelyn muttered.

"Isabel, it's been an hour." He tilted his head hopefully. "Please tell me you've had enough of this kind of fun."

"I've definitely had enough," I said, still glaring at Kate. "Get me out of here."

He threw his arm around my shoulders, pulling me tight against his body. "I told you this whole thing was a bad idea."

"And I told you to make friends, not flirt with your ex-girlfriend." My tone came out harsher than I intended.

"Hey, Isabel, can I get your help?"

I turned to find Jeremy holding a nearly unconscious Sloan in his arms. "Sloan," I groaned. I had completely forgotten about her.

"I didn't let her drink more, I promise," Jeremy said urgently. "But I think the damage was already done."

"Thanks for taking care of her," I said.

"No problem. If you tell me where she's staying, I'll help get her there." He looked to me for direction and I looked to Grayson.

"The beds are all full," he said, running a hand through his hair as he quickly made a decision. He sighed loudly, "I'll take her to my room."

Jeremy transitioned her into Grayson's arms. I followed him toward the bedroom, wondering how this was going to work. He took her directly to the bed and lowered her down gently before tucking a blanket around her. If he was annoyed to have turned his bed over to a drunk girl that wasn't his girlfriend, he didn't let it show.

"I'll get her some water. Stay with her." He left without looking at me.

I wet a washcloth with cold water and placed it on her forehead. Her eyes fluttered into a half-open position. "Thanks, Izzy."

"Just get some rest, Sloan."

"Here." Grayson had returned with a glass of water and placed it on the nightstand.

"What's the plan here?" I asked gesturing to the bed. "Hoping for a threesome tonight?"

Grayson smirked. "I've never been into unconscious girls. You and Sloan can stay in here tonight. I'll crash on the couch in my office."

"You're giving up your bed?" I wanted to object, but I couldn't think of a better plan.

"It's fine." He looked at me, eyes scanning my tight dress, and he grimaced. "Okay, it's not fine, but I'll live."

"I'm sorry, Grayson. All you wanted was for us to have some time alone and I made you do the whole party thing and now we'll be apart all night." I wrapped my arms around him. "I promise I'll never make you play nice with others ever again."

He chuckled softly and folded his body around mine. "I'm glad you've learned your lesson, darling."

"I just wish I didn't have to always learn it the hard way." I tilted my head back to receive his kiss.

"You should get some rest." He was trying to sound confident in his words, but he wasn't ready to leave me yet. "Nick told me about his plan. He wants to leave tomorrow."

"What do you think?" I asked, genuinely curious. Grayson had a sharp mind and I trusted his opinion.

"I think we need all the help we can get," he said grimly. Sloan moaned in her sleep, snapping Grayson from his deep thoughts. He forced a weak smile and kissed my cheek. "We'll talk more in the morning."

As he was walking away, every part of me wanted to run after him. In fact, I was taking a step in his direction when Sloan groaned loudly and made a noise that sounded like she might choke. I hurried to her instead and the door closed behind Grayson.

With great effort, I managed to get Sloan out of her party

dress and into my sweatpants and t-shirt. I rewet the wash-cloth and wiped down her face and neck and placed a small trashcan next to the bed. Whenever her eyes fluttered open, I forced her to drink some water. It took two hours for her to stop groaning and dry-heaving. After a while, she was even able to have small conversations with me. When she finally fell into a deep sleep that couldn't be mistaken for uncon-sciousness, I rolled her onto her side and stood.

My own dress was becoming impossibly uncomfortable. I kicked off Trina's heels and reached a hand to the back of my shoulders to start unzipping the dress and froze. The party was winding down and it had been a few hours since Grayson had left. He was probably asleep in his office by now, but there was a chance...

The door to Grayson's office was just a few feet down the hall and I approached slowly, careful not to make the floor-boards creak. As much as I was hoping he would still be awake, I didn't want to wake him up if he was already asleep. I hesitated at the door, putting my hand to the cold wood. I'll just knock once, softly, I said to myself. Before I could form a fist, the door flew open.

Grayson was wide awake, but he'd stripped down to just his boxer-briefs. They didn't leave much to imagination as I appraised him with hungry eyes. He stepped back from the open doorway without saying a word and I moved inside. Only when he'd closed the door behind me did I say, "I made you a promise earlier tonight."

"Did you?" he smiled in curiosity. "Refresh my memory, please."

"I promised to let you take this dress off me," I said, turning around and pulling my hair over my shoulder to give him clear access to the zipper, "and to let you touch me wherever you want for as long as you want."

"How could I have forgotten a promise like that?" he said in a shaking exhale. His fingers brushed my bare neck.

Very gently, he worked the zipper down an inch at a time until I almost ripped the fabric from my skin. When the zipper stopped just above the curve of my butt, Grayson's lips touched the back of my neck and began a slow and torturous descent along my spine. As he slowly dropped to his knees, his hands moved up and down my thighs.

"Turn around, darling," he whispered hoarsely.

I did as he asked, letting my hair fall around my face like a curtain as I looked down at him. He inched up the hem of my dress, moving it up over the curves of my hips. Now, his soft lips moved up my inner thighs and I moaned in agony. His lips were the very best kind of torture. While he was preoccupied with removing my underwear, I used my last remaining control to yank the dress over my head.

I stood completely naked in front of him, his mouth eagerly exploring skin that only his lips had ever touched. He closed his eyes briefly and then looked up at me and said, "You are just so beautiful, Isabel. Your beauty shatters me and I'm so completely yours."

I dropped to my knees, my heart racing. Grayson's study was cooler than his bedroom and I was shivering despite the consuming fire burning under my skin. "It's my turn to appreciate your beauty," I said, kissing his chest. He buried a hand in my hair and his fingers twisted deeper as I kissed lower and lower. It was impossible to strip his boxer briefs away in our current position, so I said, "I need you to stand, sweetheart."

He did as I asked and I moved quickly until he was just as naked as me, just as exposed. When I touched the newly exposed skin, his entire body shuddered. In a quick motion, he pulled me to my feet and backed me over to the couch. I was on my back with him on top of me before I could even breathe.

A wave of dark hair fell over his forehead and I brushed it away with the tips of my fingers before moving them over his cheek, along his jaw, stopping at his lips. Those lips that could send quakes through every inch of my body. "I love you so much," I said, the words coming on so suddenly that I had to get them out before they broke me wide open. "So, so much."

He pressed his forehead against mine, gold eyes sparkling just an inch in front of mine. A smile dazzled across his perfect lips. "I had no idea it could feel so amazing having my heart explode," he said before kissing me so incredibly sweetly that all I ever wanted to taste for the rest of my life was his lips. With his lips still pressed to mine, he said, "I love you, darling. More than you'll ever know."

10

The couch was much smaller than Grayson's bed, but after an adjustment that had me laying on top of Grayson, we were both eventually able to fall asleep. I woke up twice during the night to check on Sloan, pulling on Grayson's sweater and hoping that Sloan wouldn't open her eyes and notice.

"How is she?" Grayson asked when I returned after my second visit.

"Snoring," I said with a laugh. When I tried to lay down, Grayson held up a hand. "What?"

"I'm not going to be the only one of us that's naked," he said, pointing to the sweater. "Get rid of that."

I grinned. "Make me."

He nearly ripped the sweater as he tore it from my body. "Better," he said with a satisfied smirk as he ran a hand over my bare chest.

"It's cold in here," I complained.

Grayson turned onto his side, making more room for me on the couch. He eased me down next to him and wrapped his body around mine. "Better?" he asked, nestling his face into the curve of my neck. His breath was hot on my skin.

"Much," I murmured with my eyes closed. "For the record, this is better than any date I've ever been on."

He laughed and kissed my neck. "Same."

I was so relaxed in his arms that my body felt weightless. I was sure that if he wasn't holding me, tethering me to the couch, I would just float away. When his head jerked away, the movement was so sudden my heart jumped.

"Did you remember to lock the door?" he asked.

Before I could reply, it flew open. There was nowhere for me to go, no way for me to hide. No blankets, no clothes easily within reach. Just Dorian and Nick standing in the open doorway.

"Geez, this again?" Dorian's voice was exasperated, but his eyes were hungry as they roamed over my exposed skin. "Don't you two ever do anything else?"

Nick had gone still as stone, eyes fixed on a wall to the side. I thought about curling up, hiding my body as much as I could. But what was the point? Nick had already seen all of me and now so had Dorian. I had seen all of him, too.

"What the hell do you want, Dorian?" I said, calmly sitting up. Grayson did the same, watching me in surprise.

His cocky smile faltered. "One of my weres is missing. Jeremy. He was last seen with one of the vampires."

"Beth," Nick said, eyes flicking to me for just a second.

I grabbed Grayson's sweater from the floor and pulled it on. Then I found Grayson's pants and handed them to him. He stood and pulled them on. "Jeremy and Beth were together and now you can't find them? Forgive me, but isn't there a chance that they are just *together*?" I added extra emphasis to my words and Nick flinched.

"No," he said forcefully, eyes like fire as they bore into mine. "Beth isn't like you. She doesn't sleep around."

The words were so unexpected, they cut like a knife straight into my heart. It took a split second for the anger to set in and by then, it was too late. Grayson had already taken two steps forward and punched Nick right in the nose. Nick's entire body flew back, crashing into the wall. Dorian purposefully took a step out of the way, a large grin looking maniacal on his face.

"Grayson!" I hurried forward and tried to grab his arm, but he had already used it to hit Nick again, this time in the jaw.

Nick shoved Grayson away and spit bright red blood onto the floor. I stepped between them, holding my arms out.

"Get out of the way, Isabel," Grayson said, eyes wild with anger.

"Stop it, Grayson." I put both hands on his chest. "You're better than this."

"This is my house and you will not talk about Isabel like that." Grayson's hands were still clenched into fists and I was sure that if I moved, he would take another swing at Nick.

Nick spit again and glared at Grayson with equal hostility. I felt him moving closer behind me. "If you try to hit me again, it will be the last thing you do."

I took one hand away from Grayson and put it on Nick's chest. "Back off, Nick. If you keep talking, I'm going to hit you myself."

"Go ahead, Iz. It can't possibly hurt more than what you've already done to me." His anger shifted from Grayson to me. Now, I could see the hurt beneath the anger. He'd been acting so normally lately, even hooking up with Beth, and I'd just assumed he was over us.

"Nick," I struggled to find more words. "I'm sorry, but you have to find a way to accept this. Our circumstances don't give us the luxury of being able to avoid seeing each other."

"Whatever." Nick's guard was back in place. "Just put some clothes on that don't make you look like a prostitute. I can hardly look at you right now."

Grayson growled and started forward again. My hand was still on his chest and as I held him back, a burning sensation made my hand ache. Grayson looked down in surprise. Horrified, I realized that I was doing the same thing to him that I had done to Logan.

"No!" I yelled, yanking my hand away. I looked at him frantically. "I'm so sorry. Please say you are okay."

"I'm fine," he said, still looking at the spot where my hand had been.

"What the hell just happened?" Dorian said, glancing wildly between the two of us.

Grayson gave me a warning look. "It was nothing. Isabel and I will put some clothes on and then we'll help you find Jeremy and Beth."

"That wasn't nothing," Nick said, looking worried.

"Just go, Nick," I snapped. I was afraid that if I had to stop Grayson from hitting him again, I might be able to control whatever was happening in my hands.

Nick gave me a long look that was filled with at least a dozen conflicting emotions. When I refused to hold eye contact with Nick, he stormed out of the room.

Dorian followed at a slower pace. "As always, Jones, thanks for the show." His eyes scanned my body one more time in a purposeful way. "Looks like your body isn't the only killer thing about you."

Grayson gave him a shove through the doorway and slammed the door after him. I looked down at my hand and flexed my fingers. All traces of the heat were gone. "Grayson, are you sure I didn't hurt you?"

He came over and put a finger to my lips. "Not now," he said, barely audible. "I'm fine."

I nodded, relieved. When he took my hand, though, I feverishly tried to yank it away. He was stronger than me and he put it on his chest.

"No," I said, shaking my head in panic.

"It's fine," he whispered. "You can touch me."

Surprisingly, my hand remained a normal temperature. The heat did not return. I swallowed hard and closed my eyes. "I'm sorry."

"I'm fine," he repeated, pulling me into his arms. He held onto me until my heart slowed to a normal rhythm. "Let's get dressed," he said, slowly releasing me. "I can't believe Dorian has seen you like this twice now."

"He's a were," I said. "Nudity is their usual state. I'm sure it's not a big deal for him."

"Have you ever seen you naked?" Grayson said with a smirk.

I slapped his arm. "Stop looking at me like that."

"It really can't be helped," he said as he ushered me from the room. Sloan was still snoring softly in Grayson's bed and she didn't even flinch as we pulled on our clothes. I went with black leggings and a black sweater while Grayson just added a gray sweater to the jeans he was already wearing.

"You have sex hair," I told him, reaching up to smooth down the waves.

"Whose fault is that?" he teased, taking my hand to lead me down the hallway.

"Hey." I tugged his hand, pulling him to a stop. "You can't hit Nick again, Grayson. No matter how much he deserves it."

Grayson frowned at me. "Why are you protecting that asshole? If anyone else said those things about you, I would do much worse than just punch them."

"I don't need you to defend me," I said sternly, dropping his hand.

"I didn't punch him for you," Grayson said. "I punched him for me, because he was saying shitty things about the woman I love."

I sighed. It was hard to be firm with him when he was pouting so adorably. "You're impossible," I said, exasperated. I stormed past him.

"I believe you meant to say irresistible." Grayson sidled up next to me, snaking an arm around my waist.

"That too," I muttered as his fingers slid under my sweater. I caught his hand before he could do any further damage. "Not now, Parker."

We were back in the main party room and the destruction was shocking. It was almost as bad as when a bunch of vampires had been slaughtered during our battle with Liam's clan. "Your vamps are disgusting," I said, kicking away an empty blood bag.

"Haven't I been telling you since you got to town that all vamps are disgusting?" Dorian said from his seat on the couch.

"Have you forgotten that deal we made where you're never supposed to talk to her?" Grayson snarled.

"That was before we'd seen each other naked," Dorian said with a sly smile in my direction.

Nick grunted from where he was leaning against the wall, next to the large picture window. "Don't feel so special. She's not exactly discriminatory about who gets to see her naked these days."

I caught Grayson's arm immediately. "Nick, shut up. Dorian, make this quick."

"You already know almost everything we know. Jeremy and Beth were last seen at the party, about the exact time the two of you disappeared with the witch. No one has seen them since." Dorian almost sounded bored.

"How do you know they are missing? They could've just gone somewhere else for the night." I braced myself for a strong reaction from Nick given how he had responded to a similar suggestion earlier.

"Beth and I had plans for later this evening," Nick said. "She wouldn't have left the party without telling me."

"What kind of plans?" I said before I could stop myself.

"Please, spare us the details." Dorian was enjoying our awkward exchange. "They had sex plans, Jones."

I glared at him. "Is that also how you know Jeremy is missing? Did he bail on your booty call?"

"No, but his girlfriend can't find him. Jeremy would never go off with another girl." Dorian finally looked a little bothered by our conversation. "He's as loyal as they come. Kind of like him." Dorian nodded at Grayson.

It was the closest Dorian had ever come to complimenting Grayson and I could feel his muscles tense under my hand. I said, "Jeremy helped us get Sloan to bed. What did he do after that?"

"I saw him talking to Kate," Nick said.

"Kate?" Grayson frowned. "Why did you invite her to the party, Anderson? You don't even like her."

Dorian stood. "I didn't invite her. Rockson did."

"I most certainly did not," Nick said. "She told me Parker invited her."

"None of you invited her?" I said, suddenly very aware

that all three men had slept with the same woman. It was such a strange thing to realize that I nearly laughed out loud.

"I admit that sounds suspicious, but there's no way Kate got a vamp and a were out the door against their will all by herself," Nick said. "Besides, I don't remember seeing Beth anywhere near Kate."

Grayson ran a hand over the back of his neck. "Why would she go after Jeremy and Beth? That doesn't make any sense."

"Maybe it does," Dorian said, brow furrowed. "Kate must've known that Rockson was hooking up with Beth, so taking her would be a nice form of payback for the stunt he pulled in the barn."

"And by stunt, you mean preventing me from becoming your plaything?" I said with extra venom in my words.

"Settle down," he said.

Nick sounded annoyed when he asked, "What about Jeremy? What's his connection to any of us?"

"He was flirting with the witch," Dorian said. "Kate hasn't been around us enough to know which groupings from last night were real or just drunken hookups. She probably figured she could get back at Isabel by taking the witch's boyfriend."

"Is Kate really that evil?" I said.

"Yes," all three of them replied at once.

"And all three of you slept with her?" I shook my head in disgust. "Men."

Dorian smirked. "She's also really hot and good in the sack. The evil is easier to ignore when she's riding you like a cowgirl."

Grayson and Nick both looked like they wanted to tear Dorian's head off. I thought about letting them, but then we'd have a leaderless pack of wolves living with us. That wouldn't end well.

"Alright, well I'm done talking to you," I said. "In the morning, Sloan should be able to help us do some kind of spell to locate them. In the meantime, I'm going to get some sleep and I'd really appreciate it if the two of you would leave me the hell alone."

"Is she always this sassy?" Dorian asked Grayson.

"You have no idea," Grayson answered, surprising all of us.

He followed me out of the room, staying just a step behind as I wound my way through the twisting hallways. Neither of us spoke and I was happy for the silence. It had been a long night and I was thoroughly exhausted.

"Oh," Grayson said when I walked past his office. "You're, uh, not staying with me?"

"I really need to sleep, Grayson," I said, stopping outside his bedroom door. "If I follow you in there, I doubt we'll be doing much sleeping."

"Isabel, I can control myself for a few hours," he said, looking offended.

"If I sleep in here," I said, putting my hand on the door, "you won't have to control yourself. I'll have removed the temptation."

He nodded slowly, looking pained. "Sure, if that's what you want to do."

"Why are you looking at me like I just stomped on your heart?" I said.

"Don't worry about it. Get some rest." He leaned in to kiss me, but I put up a hand to stop him.

"Tell me what's wrong," I insisted.

Grayson turned his head away from me, looking almost embarrassed. "I won't be able to sleep," he said softly.

"Really?" I gawked at him.

"I've been a terrible sleeper for years. I think I'd just gotten used to it. But then after that first night you slept in my bed, it was like every part of me relaxed and I just... slept. More than I'd slept in years." He finally turned his eyes back to me.

"Okay, let's go." I covered the five feet to his office with determined steps.

"Isabel, really, that's not necessary. You'll sleep better in the bedroom," he protested.

I shook my head. "No, I won't. I sleep better with you, too, Grayson. Now come on, I'm exhausted."

"I owe you one," he said as he pushed the door open.

"You really, really do," I said with an elaborate sigh. "This is going to be so torturous for me."

"Cute," Grayson said, squeezing my shoulder. This time, he made sure the door was locked before settling onto the couch. I waited for him to open his arms and then I curled myself around him. His chest was the perfect pillow, his arms the softest blanket. Within five minutes of closing my eyes, we were both asleep.

11

"Are you sure?"

Sloan nodded, eyes still closed. "Completely sure."

Nick looked doubtful despite her assurance. "That can't be."

"Why not?" I asked and I was rewarded with a scowl.

We were sitting in the same room as the previous night, though it was much cleaner this morning. I'd woken with a surprising amount of energy and had cleaned up most of the disaster caused by the party before showering and waking Sloan for some spell casting.

I sat between Sloan and Grayson on one couch with Nick and Dorian across from us. I doubted either of them had gotten much sleep, but they looked far better than myself and Sloan. Human hangovers were nothing to mess with. Grayson, as always, looked perfect.

"Beth isn't a traitor. She wouldn't have willingly followed Kate into Liam's lair." Nick's knees bounced in agitation.

Sloan opened her eyes. "You misinterpreted what I said."

"You said that you located Beth and Jeremy and they are

in the same place where Liam was keeping you. Then you said that both of them are walking around freely and they aren't being held hostage." Nick had turned his scowl to Sloan. "How else should I interpret that?"

"If you hadn't known I was compelled, wouldn't you have assumed I had willingly chosen to help Liam fight against you?" Sloan said, not at all intimidated.

"Vampires can't be compelled," Grayson said in a deep, rough voice. It was the first sign that maybe he hadn't recovered as easily as I had thought.

"Not like humans, but they are still susceptible to magic," Sloan said. "I could make you cluck like a chicken right now if I wanted to."

I turned to her. "Really?"

"Sure." She shrugged. "I mean, I haven't tried that particular spell yet, but it's just about mind control and that's generally simple enough."

"Are you telling me that Liam found a way to control other supernatural creatures?" Grayson asked with a touch of panic in his voice.

"That would be my guess. But he wouldn't be able to do it himself. Vampires can't wield magical abilities. If he's performing mind control, that means he's found himself another witch." Sloan frowned. "A powerful one, too. My aunt has taught me everything I know and she's as powerful as a witch can get."

Dorian turned to Grayson. "If Liam has his own witch, there's nothing stopping him from attacking us again."

"There might be something else," Grayson said. He didn't look at me, but I knew he was thinking about my newly developed power. Had Liam sensed that power within me when he touched me? Is that why he had let me go so easily? "We don't have much choice anymore. If Liam has another witch working for him, we need to know for sure."

"Would your uncle's wife be able to get confirmation for us?" I asked Nick. My head was pounding and I wanted a cup of coffee more than anything.

"I think so," he said.

"Then we stick with the original plan," Grayson said. "Isabel, Nick, and myself will meet with the uncle and witch."

"Excuse me?" Sloan said. "You can't possibly be planning to leave me alone in this vampire den."

Grayson stared at her. "You are perfectly safe here, Sloan."

"Easy for you to say," she muttered.

"She'll come with us," I said.

"Isabel." Grayson shot me a warning glance.

"We might need her," I said, cutting off any protest. "We don't know if Nick's uncle will be an ally. We have no idea if his wife is a friendly witch or one that will try to kill us. The best way to guarantee our safety is by bringing our own witch arsenal."

Nick nodded. "She's right."

"I'm always right," I said.

"Fine." Grayson threw up his hands. "Why do I even bother anymore? This clan is clearly a democracy now."

"Stop pouting," I teased and was rewarded with a harsh glare. I had gone too far. "Grayson, you know this is the best thing for us to do."

He ignored me. "We'll stick with the original schedule and leave just before dark. We can't risk too much sun exposure outside of the falls."

"And vampires are supposed to be so badass," Dorian said with a sad shake of his head.

"Dorian, we're done here. Feel free to go annoy someone else." Grayson's heart wasn't in his reproach.

"If we're not leaving until later, I'm going to find some coffee." I stood and waited a second for the throbbing in my head to dull.

"I'm going to run home and collect some of my things," Sloan said.

Grayson nodded. "Everyone meet back here by 5:00."

I was already on my way to the kitchen. I was sure that I would be able to think much clearer after a cup, or pot, of coffee. It only took a couple minutes of searching for me to realize that I wasn't going to get my fix in the mansion.

"Do you really not have any coffee? Are you really going to disappoint me this morning?" I asked Grayson when he came into the room.

"Sorry, darling. Vampires don't really need caffeine." He leaned back against the counter and smiled. "Plenty of blood in the fridge, though."

"Gee, thanks." I paused. "I haven't seen you drink any blood lately. Have you developed a platelet disorder?"

His smile faltered. "I've been drinking enough. Don't worry about me."

"You're lying," I said, proud of myself before being able to tell. "Why?"

He looked away. "I don't want you to see me that way."

"I've seen you drink blood, Grayson. You were drinking it the very first time we met at Mack's," I reminded him.

"That was before," he said with a quick shake of his head. "It's different now."

"How is it different? You're still a vampire. You still need to drink blood." I moved closer to him, putting my arms around his waist. He kept his eyes locked on the wall. "Look at me, Grayson."

He did, with an urgency that made my heart ache. "Isabel, when I'm with you, I don't feel like a vampire. You make me feel like a man and I forget about this other side of me. But if I so much as think about drinking blood around you, it all comes crashing back."

"I don't care that you drink blood, Grayson. Being a vampire is just a part of who you are and I love every part of you." I searched his eyes to see if I was getting through to him. He looked unconvinced. "Look at it this way, I'm pretty much a nightmare to be around until I've had my coffee, but you still love me right now, don't you?"

"Coffee and blood are not the same thing, darling." A tiny curl of his lips made my heart thump happily as he put his arms around my shoulders. "But I appreciate your attempt to make me feel better."

"I just don't want you to starve yourself for me," I said. My head dropped until I was looking at his chest, hesitating over my next words. "Have you ever... I mean, would you ever... consider...drinking from a human?"

His arms tightened. "No."

"No you haven't or no you wouldn't?" I still couldn't look him in the eye.

"I haven't and I wouldn't," he said firmly.

"Not even if the human wanted you to do it?" I said. I'd heard rumors about people that lived in the nearby towns who let vampires feed on them for money. I had no idea if it was true, but I suspected that it was.

"Why are you asking me this, Isabel?" Grayson sounded more than a little suspicious.

I took a deep breath and let it out slowly. "Blood from the vein is better, isn't it?"

"That's a loaded question," he said.

"It tastes better. You can't deny it, I know that's true. I've heard your vampires discuss it amongst themselves." I wasn't sure why he was being so elusive when that information was quite well known. "It also makes you stronger, doesn't it?"

"Yes," he said quietly.

I finally allowed my eyes to meet his. "Would you ever consider drinking from me, if I asked you to?"

"What?" his mouth dropped open and he sputtered. "Why are you asking me that?"

"Just answer me. Would you ever drink from me?" I could see the horror in his eyes. "Not to kill me, obviously. But for strength and for... pleasure."

"No, Isabel. A thousand times no. I will never, ever drink from you, not even if my life depends on it." He stared so hard into my eyes that I could almost feel them burning from the intensity.

"Not even if I beg you?" I said.

Grayson dropped his arms and pushed me away. "Stop, Isabel. This isn't something to joke about."

"I'm not joking," I said. "I trust you, Grayson. I trust you to take just enough blood to satisfy yourself without hurting me."

"Stop," he said again, closing his eyes. "I'm not having this conversation with you."

"Fine." I sighed and stepped back. "But if you aren't going to drink from me, you need to drink the blood bags. You're too weak."

His gold eyes flew open. "You don't have to worry about me, Isabel. I've been a vampire for longer than you've even known vampires exist."

"I don't have a choice. I have to worry about you." I shrugged. "I love you."

His eyes were unquestionably sad when he said, "I know. I should've warned you not to do that."

"I'm going to find some coffee," I said after taking a shaking breath. "I could use the fresh air and caffeine."

"Can I come with you?" he asked hopefully.

"I'd like that." I smiled, but couldn't look him in the eyes. I was embarrassed to have even started such a conversation with him. Grayson would never feed from me, I knew that. Still, part of me wondered how much of his true nature he was hiding to protect me.

Grayson insisted on driving me downtown for breakfast, even opening the car door for me. I teased him about it and he just shrugged and asked if I had a problem with my boyfriend being nice to me. He held my hand on the way into the diner and I gave him a suspicious look.

"Don't be so paranoid," he said. "Am I not allowed to hold your hand in public?"

When he reached across the table after we were seated and took my hand again, I narrowed my eyes at him. "Why are you being so weird?"

"I'm not being weird," he said defensively. "Why are you being so jumpy?"

"Because we don't do this, Grayson," I said, gesturing to our interlocked hands.

"Just because we *haven't* done something, doesn't mean it's weird if we start doing it." He squeezed my hand for extra emphasis.

The waitress came to take our orders and I was surprised when Grayson ordered a coffee. "Explain yourself, Parker," I said with an accusatory glare. "You said vampires don't need coffee."

"We don't," he said with a smirk. "But I didn't want you to drink alone. Besides, I like the taste of coffee."

"Vampires are so weird," I muttered.

Grayson just smiled. "How's school going?"

"How's school going?" I repeated back to him, flabber-gasted. Suddenly, it hit me. "Are we on a *date* right now?"

"Must not be a very good one if you just figured it out," he said with a laugh. His thumb traced a slow circle over the back of my hand and the tingles that tiny movement caused reached all the way to the center of my chest.

"Is this because of our conversation in the kitchen?" I said softly.

He looked away, out the window. "You freaked me out a little bit, Isabel. You're my girlfriend. You should be asking me to take you to the movies or to prom, not to drink your blood. Just because my life is dark and disgusting doesn't mean our relationship has to be that way."

"Hey." I waited for him to look at me. "There is nothing about you that I find dark or disgusting, Grayson. I just want you to be yourself with me, completely. I want to experience all of you, not just the easy, sexy parts."

"Do you know that I'm happier right now, sitting in this café holding your hand, than I ever was before I met you." His normally deep voice had taken on a breathy tone. "Can you even imagine how unbelievable I feel in those moments when we're doing more than holding hands? You don't need to worry about doing anything to enhance my pleasure, darling. I'm already maxed out."

"That's really sweet, Grayson, and I love you for saying that, but you can't deny that my blood could make you stronger," I whispered. "You can't deny that we would both be better off if you were as strong as possible."

"I'm strong enough," he said.

He let go of my hand as the waitress arrived with our order. Grayson was sticking with just coffee, but I'd ordered breakfast as well. He sat quietly, watching me eat and drinking his coffee slowly.

"I don't know if I like you watching me eat," I said.

"I can watch someone else eat instead," he offered with an adorable grin. "If you're planning on staying in this relationship for long, you probably should get used to this."

"If?" I froze with my coffee halfway to my mouth.

"It will always be a choice for you, Isabel. I will never take you or our relationship for granted. I don't doubt your love for me right now, but you're still very young and you've got a whole life ahead of you." He looked hard into his coffee mug. "One day, your feelings for me might change. If that happens, I'll understand."

He words nearly broke my heart. Without thinking, I kicked him hard in the shin.

"Hey!" His head jerked up and he glared at me. My kick hadn't hurt him physically, but his pride was wounded.

"This isn't a choice for me," I said determinedly. "I love you."

"Not that long ago, you loved Nick," he said without a hint of jealousy or malice.

A cold chill ran through me. Those harsh words that Nick had thrown at me had seemed nothing more than childish attacks, but now I could see that they'd had a surprising effect. They'd made Grayson question my feelings for him.

"Not the way I love you," I said. This time, I reached over and took his hand, prying it away from the mug. His eyes were hopeful when he looked at me. "Do you believe me?"

"Did you ever call him sweetheart?" Grayson asked, but his eyes said that he already knew the answer to his question.

"No. *You* are my only sweetheart." I squeezed his hand, hard. "Now and always."

He slid me an easy wink. "I *knew* you liked me."

"Guilty." I finally took a sip of the coffee, giving myself a few seconds to swallow down my emotions along with the caffeine. "In other news, what do you really think of Nick's plan to meet up with his uncle?"

"I think I'd like it better if it was anyone else's plan," he said with a grimace. "He was really out of line with those things he said to you."

"He's hurt," I said with a shrug. "He's not handling it well, but neither of us can change that. Fighting with him is only going to make it worse."

"That's very mature of you," he said with a sheepish smile. "I'll try to follow your lead going forward."

"Good." I looked at my half-eaten breakfast. "If Liam really does have a witch working for him, we aren't going to be safe for much longer."

Grayson watched me silently for a few seconds. "I've been thinking about that. We might have another way to fight Liam."

"A way that doesn't involve us dying?"

"You were able to kill Logan with just one touch," Grayson said. "If we could figure out how to harness your power, maybe it could be used to stop an entire vampire army."

"I think that's just wishful thinking, Grayson," I said. "I don't even know how to instigate the power, let alone control it."

He leaned forward. "I have a theory about that. Both times you used the power, you were in imminent danger from a supernatural being."

"Not the second time," I corrected him. "I never thought you were going to hurt me."

"Fine, but you thought I was going to hurt Nick and you

were trying to protect him, right?" Grayson's face darkened just a little.

I nodded. "Okay, so I can leverage the power when I, or something I'm trying to protect, is threatened by someone supernatural? Let's say you are right about that, it still doesn't address how I'm going to learn to control that power."

"You'll learn the same way you learned how to hunt. Practice." He took the bill from the waitress and handed it back to her with some cash.

"Did you just buy me breakfast?" I said with a smile.

"I told you this was a date." He flashed his trademark grin at me. "Think there's any chance I'll get a kiss at the end of the date?"

"There's a good chance you'll get a whole lot more than a kiss if you keep smiling at me that way." I gave him what I hoped was a sexy look.

He jumped to his feet still holding my hand and pulled me up. "You're ready to go, right?"

"What's the hurry, Parker?" I teased with a laugh as he hurried outside.

"Walk now, talk later," he said, an arm encircling my waist as he ushered me toward the car. Two of his fingers snaked under my shirt.

"Hey, wait." I pulled to a sudden stop. "I should've said something earlier, but I'm busy this morning. They're having a memorial for Elena at the school at 10:00."

His smile vanished instantly. "Right, well, that's obviously important. Do you want me to go with you?"

"No, that's not necessary," I said out of habit.

"You know, I've thrown the doors to my world wide open for you," he said, sounding sad, "and you haven't even cracked a window into your world for me."

I wanted to argue with him, but he was right. In the time that I'd known Grayson, the closest he'd come to my life was picking me up at school.

"Come with me," I said.

"If you don't want me there, I'm not going to force you to let me go," he said.

I put a hand on his chest. "Please? You were right, I haven't let you into my life and I need to fix that. I *want* to fix it. Please, come with me today."

"Are you sure?" He looked at me without a hint of pressure.

"I'm sure. It's going to be a rough morning and it will be nice to have you by my side." I gave him a quick kiss and added, "Plus, I wouldn't mind showing off my hot boyfriend. There's a couple of mean girls at school that are going to die when they see your gorgeous face."

He cleared his throat, embarrassed. "We should go now if you want to have enough time to change before the service."

"Thanks for the date," I said, pulling his head down to kiss him again. "Maybe next time we can go dancing."

"I have very fond memories of dancing with you." Grayson's eyes sparkled with the memory. "That was the first time you ever looked at me like you were seeing a man and not just a vampire. It was the first time I ever thought that you might like me."

"We've come a long way since then," I said, skimming my fingers over his neck and into the hair at the back of his head.

"I don't know, some things haven't changed at all," he said, putting his lips close to my ear. He was holding me very similarly to how he had held me that night at Mack's. The only difference was that we weren't swaying to any music. "Except that I'm even more in love with you."

"And that whole thing where we have sex now," I joked.

"Yeah alright, things are a little better now." He kissed his way from my ear to my lips, taking his time until his tongue danced playfully over mine. Grayson knew seemingly a hundred different ways to kiss me and each one was just as magnificent as the last. He pulled away a full minute later and said, "Let's go home, darling."

"Home," I agreed, reveling how easily that word passed through my lips. Home wasn't the mansion for me, not really. Home was wherever Grayson was and it was the only place I ever wanted to be.

12

"Where are the mean girls?" Grayson whispered to me.

We'd made it through the memorial service and now we were all gathered on the football field to release balloons with messages for Elena and the other murdered girls. The whole thing was a little cheesy for me, but others seemed to find solace in writing their messages, so who was I to judge?

"One of them is right there," I said, nodding to the blonde just a few feet away. Susie flipped her hair and turned at exactly that moment, looking very much like a supermodel. Unlike the other mourners, she didn't look the least bit sad as the girls on either side of her laughed at something she said. Susie's eyes landed on Grayson, catching him staring at her. She smiled broadly at him.

Grayson continued to stare, giving her the same unreadable expression that always drove me crazy. She took it as encouragement and started in our direction.

"This should be fun," I muttered.

"Hi," she said in a sultry voice. "I'm Susie. Are you the new baseball coach?"

"No," Grayson said coldly. I stifled a laugh.

Susie tilted her head and smiled. "Well, I know you aren't a student. I'd remember a face like yours."

Grayson scanned her once, still unimpressed. "I'm here with Isabel."

"Isabel?" Susie noticed me for the first time. Her perfect nose wrinkled. She noticed our interlocked hands for the first time. "Really?"

Again, Grayson just stared. I knew better than anyone how unnerving his stare could be and I almost felt bad for Susie.

"Are we done here?" Grayson said, turning to me. The look he gave me was nothing like the look he had given her.

"Yeah, we're done." I smiled as he leaned down, kissing me softly on the lips. He wasn't doing it to prove a point to Susie. I could tell from the look in his eyes that he had completely forgotten about her. "Have you seen Nick or Sloan?"

"I really wish you wouldn't say his name when I'm kissing you," Grayson said with a grimace. "It's a real mood killer."

"And the memorial service for four dead girls wasn't a mood killer?" I said.

He shrugged. "I *am* a vampire."

"It's a good thing I know you are joking." I caught a glimpse of Sloan over his shoulder and Nick was standing next to her.

I had been surprised when Nick had insisted on tagging along, but I had forgotten that he knew both Logan and Elena. Nick and Logan had been friends for most of their lives until recently, and Nick had grown up around both of them. He felt it was only right to pay respects to the family and even Grayson couldn't argue with that.

"I found them," I said with a slight nod of my head in their direction.

"Goody," Grayson grumbled.

I rolled my eyes. "Grow up, Parker. We're about to take a road trip with him, so you better get used to having him around."

"As long as he doesn't run his mouth about you, I'll be fine." Grayson looked annoyed as he remembered the terrible things Nick had said about me. I was still reeling from his attacks myself.

"I don't need you to defend me," I said. "Just let me handle my ex and when it's time, I'll let you handle yours."

"Kate and I broke up five years ago," Grayson said, as if that made a difference. "That's not exactly comparable to the situation with Nick."

"At least Nick is fighting alongside us and not against us," I said with extra annoyance. "Your girlfriend wouldn't hesitate to kill any of us."

"*Ex*-girlfriend." Grayson's eyes narrowed. "You do remember that *you* are my girlfriend, don't you?"

"What was she saying to you when I stumble upon your intimate moment during the party?" I said, feeling childish but asking the question anyway.

Grayson laughed. "Are you jealous of Kate?"

"She was touching you," I said. "As you just pointed out, Kate is your *ex*-girlfriend, so why was she touching you?"

"Because she was hoping you would see us and overreact." Grayson smirked. "Not sure why she thought that would happen."

"Don't be a smartass, Grayson." I stepped around him, headed for Nick and Sloan.

Grayson's hand closed around my arm. "Kate told me not to trust Nick."

"Nick?" I whispered. "That's ridiculous."

"Is it?" Grayson raised an eyebrow. His eyes darted away briefly before flicking back to mine. "We'll talk later."

Nick and Sloan were walking in our direction. I forced my face to relax and even smiled at Grayson. "Play nice," I said.

Grayson's hand dropped from my arm. "I will if he does."

"We should get out of here," Sloan said, her bloodshot eyes scanning the field. "I don't like how exposed we are."

"There's almost no chance Liam is here," I said, hoping that was true.

"You didn't think he'd be at the dance either," Sloan said pointedly.

She had a point. Grayson put his hand on my back and nudged me forward. "I agree with Sloan. It was dumb for us to come here."

"It would be dumb for Liam to attempt anything while Sloan is with us," I said.

Nick also appeared antsy and he mimicked Grayson's posture, pushing Sloan forward. "We can argue over stupidity later. Let's just get out of here."

I noticed the stiff set of Grayson's jaw and Nick's flared nostrils. They were reacting to something that Sloan and I couldn't detect.

"What's happening?" I asked Grayson as Nick and Sloan navigated their way through the crowd just a few feet ahead of us.

"Whatever has been happening with the protective magic in town over the last few weeks has suddenly escalated," he said, moving closer to me until it felt like his entire body was moving me forward. "I can feel the sun draining me."

"Really?" My eyes were wide when I looked at him. I'd

never seen Grayson affected by anything, least of all the sun. "Are you going to be okay?"

He nodded his head stiffly. "We just need to get back to the mansion."

For once, I barely noticed that Grayson was driving at least double the speed limit. Even though the vampires had been dealing with the fading magical protection for a while, none of us had been prepared for such a sudden shift. We had hardly stepped through the mansion's front door before being confronted by a dozen vampires demanding to know what had happened.

Grayson urged them to calm down, but the panic was palpable. I could see Grayson was straining to retain his composure. Eventually, he was able to convince them to rest until sunset when the council could regroup. It was clear from the lethargic movements of the vamps that Grayson and Nick weren't the only ones feeling the effects of the sun.

"You need to get some rest, too," I told Grayson as he paced the length of his bedroom, running a hand through his hair and muttering to himself. I had never seen him this agitated. "You'll need your strength this evening."

"I'm fine," he said without looking at me.

I pulled my legs up to my chest, curling deeper into the leather chair as I watched his regulated marching. It wasn't unusual for him to pace when he was nervous, but I'd never seen him so focused on his anxiety that he wouldn't even look at me.

"Can you tell if the other magic is gone, too?" I asked quietly. "The one protecting the humans."

Grayson nodded. "It's gone."

"Does that mean every human in the falls is in imminent danger once the sun goes down?" I wasn't able to keep the fear from my voice.

Grayson turned, almost as if he was surprised that I was there. "I don't know. Maybe."

"What do you mean, maybe?"

"Well, you've been vulnerable this whole time. The magic in this town never protected you because of your Hunter blood. When I'm around you, the desire to feed is always there, but I'm able to resist." He finally stopped pacing and came across the room to sit in the chair near mine. "Just because the humans are no longer protected, it doesn't mean the vampires have no choice."

"But you love me, Grayson," I said. "That's how you're able to resist. If this room was full of humans right now, would you be able to resist all of them?"

"Yes," he said quickly. "Vampires aren't slaves to the bloodthirst, Isabel."

I was still skeptical, but it wasn't my place to tell him how he might react. "You might be able to resist, but would all the vampires in this house make that same choice?"

"I guess we're going to find out." Grayson stared at the floor, his shoulders slumped. "We've never had to worry about this."

"Do you think Liam is responsible?" It was impossible not to make the connection given that the protective enchantment was broken just as Liam had been discovered to have a witch working for him.

"I think I'd be surprised if he wasn't responsible." He placed his elbows on his knees and dropped his head, massaging the back of his neck with one hand.

I climbed out of my chair and went over to him. "Let me," I said, stepping on the arm rest and climbing behind him. I sat on the headrest and straddled my legs on either side of his back, placing my hands on the side of his neck and working the tense muscles with my thumbs.

He started to relax almost immediately. "You really know how to use those hands."

"You need to get some rest, sweetheart. You're running on fumes." I worked my hands along his shoulders.

"This is better than any amount of rest," he said with a sigh.

I leaned down and kissed him where his neck curved into his shoulder. His skin was shockingly cool against my lips. "Are you sure you're alright?" I asked, lips still pressed against him.

"You were right this morning," he said, his voice hoarse. "I haven't been drinking enough blood."

"Why not?" I was afraid to move, afraid that he would shut down just as suddenly as he'd opened up.

"Because I don't like drinking blood when I'm with you. It almost feels like I'm cheating on you or something." He laughed dryly. "I'm sorry, that was a weird thing to say."

"It's not weird. It's how you feel." I wrapped my arms around him from behind and rested my chin on his shoulder. "I'm sorry it's hard for you, but I really do understand that you don't have a choice. You have to drink, Grayson."

He nodded. "I know."

"My offer still stands," I said softly, pushing my lips against his ear. "If you don't want to drink the other blood, you can have mine."

"No, Isabel." His shoulders tensed instantly.

"Would it really be so bad?" I asked. "We've shared everything else, Grayson. You need this to stay strong, and I'm happy to give it. I *want* to give it."

"It will change everything," he said quietly.

I smiled even though he couldn't see it. "You changed everything when you kissed me, sweetheart. And then again when you invited me into your bed. Both of those things brought us closer. Why can't this do the same thing?"

"Because with this, I could kill you." He gently extricated himself from my arms and stood. "I've never...done that, Isabel. I don't know if I can control myself."

"You've really never taken blood directly from a human?" I said, shocked.

"No. Not since Elsie, and I wasn't a vampire then." His voice was shaking. "The urge is so much stronger now, especially when I'm around you."

His words cut straight into my heart. Grayson had always made it seem like his control around me was easy. I'd had no idea he had been struggling.

"I'm sorry," I said, tears springing to my eyes. "If I've been making things hard for you, I'm sorry. I had no idea."

Grayson whirled, a blur of fluid motion as he turned to me and said, "No, don't you dare apologize. None of this is your fault, Isabel. I'd rather spend a lifetime in aching desire with you than a second of blissful peace without you."

"What if you could have both?" I said, sliding off the chair. "What if you could give into the desire with me, just enough to kill the craving? Wouldn't it be worth it to try?"

"Not if the other possibility is that I can't control myself and I kill you." Grayson's eyes were the palest shade of yellow I had ever seen.

"I'm not Elsie," I said, taking a step toward him. "I'm strong enough to stop you if you go too far."

He gave his head one firm shake and turned away. "I'm going to do as you asked and get some rest."

I watched as he shuffled over and settled onto the bed. He was still fully clothed, minus his shoes, and he settled onto his back. I had never seen Grayson so tense and I hoped my persistence hadn't added to his stress. When I perched on the edge of the mattress to study him closer, he showed no sign that he even knew I was there.

Without waiting for an invitation, I scooted over on the mattress and lay my body alongside his, just an inch away from touching. He turned his head to look at me, offering a weak smile that was the only prompting I needed. I wrapped an arm across his chest and curled a leg around him. After lightly kissing his cheek, I settled my head on his shoulder and closed my eyes.

"I love you," I said, just in case he needed the reminder.

After a long moment of silence, he replied, "I don't deserve it, but I'll take it anyway."

I waited an hour to make sure that Grayson was sleeping before making my way to his wall of books. He'd already told me to take whatever I wanted, but for some reason I didn't want him to know I was so eager to read Annie Jones' journal. In all the excitement of the day, I'd nearly forgotten that Grayson told me he had it in his library. I scanned five shelves before finding it.

The leather cover was just as worn and faded as Elias' journal, but Annie's handwriting was much neater. I took the book to the leather chair and started reading from the beginning. Unlike her brother, Annie had started her journal on her 16th birthday. I had two years of ancient drama to comb through before getting to anything relevant.

A few months after Annie's 18th birthday, she started to notice strange developments. It all started at a friend's debutante ball in a nearby town. A gentleman got a little too frisky with Annie during a dance. When she put her hand on his chest to push him away, she felt a strange heat emanating from her hand. Later that night, Elias Jones would end up staking that same guy, a vampire, in the heart out back in the garden.

Annie learned more about the supernatural world as her brother became more experienced hunting. He spent a lot of time away from the falls, traveling to nearby towns where the supernatural creatures were freely preying on humans. Annie begged to travel with her brother, and Elias eventually relented. Elias became aware of Annie's powers and he helped her control them. Soon, she was killing vampires with a simple touch of her hand while Elias looked on in wonder.

It was unclear why Elias had chosen not to document any of this in his journal, but it was clear that my own power wasn't just a fluke. Grayson's speculation about it being tied to the founding families' curse was looking to be accurate. What was less certain was why Annie's journal stopped abruptly just a few months after discovering her power.

The sun was starting to set and Grayson would be awake soon. I put the journal down and headed to the kitchen. If Grayson wasn't going to drink my blood, he needed to drink from the blood bags. Even though the idea of drinking blood still made me squeamish, I emptied one of the bags into a glass and returned to the bedroom.

Grayson was just beginning to stir, but his eyes were still closed. I set the glass on the table next to the bed and ran a hand along his jaw. "The sun will be down soon," I said. "We'll need to hit the road in a bit."

"You didn't stay in bed," he said, slowly opening his eyes.

"I wasn't tired." I glanced at the table. "I brought you something to drink. Please don't fight me on this."

"Isabel." He eyed the glass wearily.

"Grayson, you are starving yourself for no good reason." I gave him my sternest look. "I will not let you do that. I love you too much to see you suffering."

He sat up and surprised me by leaning in to kiss my cheek. "Okay."

"Okay?" I smiled triumphantly. "Really?"

"I can't say no to you," he said simply. "But I don't want you to watch me."

"I've seen you drink blood, Grayson." I put a hand on his leg. "You don't have to protect me from it."

"Just do me this favor, okay?" He gave me a weary look. "I promise to buy you a fancy coffee maker for the kitchen if you just give me a few minutes alone."

I pretended to swoon. "You really are the perfect man."

"Go." He gave me a slight nudge.

"Your wish is my command." I kissed his cheek before standing. "Take your time. I'm sure I can entertain myself for a bit."

"Don't go too far, okay?" Grayson sounded worried. "Until we know more about what is happening to this town, you should stay close."

"Sure, Dad," I called over my shoulder.

I heard him grumbling something at me, but I shut the door behind me and forced myself to keep walking down the hall. No matter how much time I spent in the mansion, it never felt like home to me and I hated every part of it except for Grayson's bedroom. It didn't help that vampires and weres lurked around every corner.

Instead of staying inside, I headed out the front door with plans to relax on the porch until Grayson came looking for me. I was surprised to find Sloan there, reading an ancient-looking book.

"Care for some company?" I asked.

She looked up and smiled. "I didn't expect to see you until after sunset."

"Grayson's been resting all afternoon," I explained,

sitting next to her on the steps. "I just finished doing some reading myself. That doesn't look like a school book."

"It's our family grimoire." Sloan closed the book and ran a hand over the worn cover. "My aunt gave it to me. I thought I'd brush up on some enchantments before we hit the road."

"Have you been out here this whole time?" I asked.

"I don't exactly have anywhere to go," she said quietly. "I didn't figure Grayson would want me hanging out in his room again."

"I'll have him assign you a room." I felt terrible for not thinking of Sloan earlier. "Hopefully, things won't stay like this forever."

She smiled. "You mean you don't want to be shacking up with your hot boyfriend in a mansion?"

"Okay, it isn't all bad," I said with a laugh. "But part of me is ready for everything to go back to normal. Remember when our biggest concern was buying a dress for the dance?"

"That feels like a lifetime ago." Sloan looked wistfully at the sunset. "When we bought those dresses, you were still dating Nick."

"Not everything was simpler back then." It seemed strange that dating Grayson, a vampire clan leader, was far easier than any of my past relationships.

Sloan turned to me. "You seem really happy with Grayson. Don't let Nick, or anyone else, make you feel bad for being with him."

"You don't think I'm crazy for falling in love with a vampire?" I asked.

"You are absolutely crazy," Sloan said with a laugh. "But I've seen the way he looks at you, Izzy. That vampire boy completely adores you. It's clear that he would never hurt you. Plus, he's absurdly beautiful. I say, go for it."

I let out a long breath. "He really is beautiful, isn't he?"

"I'd hit that," she said with an eyebrow waggle. "The vamp sex has to be amazing."

"You have no idea," I said with a sigh.

We were both laughing so hard we didn't hear the front door open. My cheeks blushed hotly when Grayson stepped onto the porch. There was no way he hadn't heard our conversation. In typical Grayson fashion, his face was unreadable.

"We should take off soon," he said, eyes darting between us.

"Is Nick awake?" I hated even saying his name to Grayson, but given we were all about to be trapped in a car for a few hours, I needed to get over it.

"Awake and as delightful as ever," he said with a frown.

Sloan jumped to her feet. "I'll work on cheering him up. We can't start this road trip off on the wrong foot."

As Sloan passed Grayson she turned and mouth the word "beautiful" with extra exaggeration, making me laugh. Grayson looked at me like I was insane.

"You look better," I said, noting the slight pink in his cheeks. The blood was already working.

"I feel better." He took Sloan's spot on the stairs. After a long pause, he tilted his head at me and smiled. "Thank you for being so insufferable."

"Anytime." I leaned against the porch railing, facing Grayson. "Are you sure you can go with us tonight? With all the changes today, shouldn't you stay here to keep an eye on things?"

Grayson's smile vanished. "I'm going with you, Isabel."

"I know that you want to, I'm asking if that's really the right thing to do." I hadn't meant for the words to come out so accusatorily.

"I'm going with you," he repeated through a clenched

jaw. "Trina and Dorian can handle things back here for one night."

"Okay," I said quickly. "You know best."

"Not always." He was frowning again.

I nudged his foot with mine. "Hey, what's wrong?"

"Is this really the life you want?" he asked, looking straight into my eyes.

I flinched, stunned by the question. "What are you talking about?"

"I want you to answer honestly. Don't worry about hurting my feelings. Do you really want to be dating a vampire and living in a dark mansion with a bunch of super-natural creatures? Do you want to be forcing your boyfriend to drink blood?" He shook his head slowly. "Because I don't want this for you, Isabel. I love you too much."

"I have no idea where this is coming from." I sat up, my heart racing. "Are you breaking up with me?"

"No. I'm telling you that I will understand if *you* want to break up with *me*. Really. I will understand." He didn't so much as blink as he stared into my soul. "All I want is for you to be happy, even if that means you have to leave me behind."

My heart was thumping so hard I worried it might jump right out of my chest. "Grayson, I've never been happier than I am with you. Why in the world would I ever want to leave that behind?"

"This is just the start," he said, gesturing to the last orange streaks in the sky. "I won't be able to walk in the light with you anymore, Isabel. Any life we have together will be in the dark. If I truly love you, how could I ask you to give up the sun for me? To give up your life for me?"

"You're not asking me," I said, grabbing his arm with

both hands. "I'm doing it willingly. I'd give up everything to be with you."

"You shouldn't have to," he said quietly. "I want to make your life better, not harder."

"You do." I placed my hand on the back of his neck and pulled his face closer to mine. "Grayson, I have no idea why you would ever think that I'm not stupidly, obsessively in love with you – with *all* of you. I've known about your vampire side from the very beginning and I love you not in spite of it, but because of it. It's part of who you are."

He closed his eyes and grimaced. "It's the worst part of me."

"There is no worst part of you, Grayson," I said firmly. "To me, you are perfect."

His eyes opened. "Sloan was right."

"About?"

"Me." Grayson touched his forehead to mine, his eyes so close that their gold flames warmed every inch of me. "I adore you, Isabel Jones."

13

"Would you stop fidgeting?" Sloan snapped.

"I can't get comfortable." Nick's knee dug into the back of my seat.

"Don't make me pull this car over," Grayson grumbled with a glance in the rearview mirror. His hands were tight on the steering wheel.

I glanced over my shoulder. "I told you to take the front seat."

"I'd rather be in the trunk," Nick said with a pointed glare at Grayson.

"We can make that happen." Grayson looked as though he was seriously considering pulling over and shoving Nick into the trunk.

We'd been on the road for two hours and nearly all that time had been spent listening to grumbles and snide comments. Sloan had attempted casual conversation a few times, but she was quickly deterred.

"Okay, I really need the two of you to knock it off," I snapped. "You're acting like childish brats."

Grayson glanced at me, at first looking as if he was about

to say something that would only further annoy me. When he saw the disgust on my face, he thought better of it and turned back to the road.

"Do you really think your uncle will be able to help?" Sloan asked, not nearly as annoyed as me. Despite the grumpy atmosphere, she was still in good spirits.

"I don't know," Nick said. "Uncle Dave hasn't really been part of my life, so I have no idea what to expect."

"Do you know anything about the woman he married?" I asked.

"All I know is that they met about four years ago and got married. She has a daughter in high school." Nick added, "And that she's a witch, obviously."

Sloan giggled. "You don't have to say it like it's a bad word."

"Like you don't stutter over the word vampire," Nick volleyed back.

I detected something in Nick's voice that I hadn't expected. He wasn't annoyed by Sloan's endless questioning, he was charmed by it. I knew Nick well enough to know when he was flirting.

"Is this our exit?" Grayson asked, oblivious to the undertones of the exchange.

"Yep." I was glad that we were almost there. "It should be just down this road."

"Are we sure it's a good idea for the four of us to approach him together?" Grayson sounded a little nervous.

Nick shifted again, kneeing me in the back. "We're about to approach a Hunter and a witch. I don't have any plans to do that alone."

"Strength in numbers," I agreed. "It's only going to take him a second to realize you're a vampire, Nick. What should I do if he tries to stake you?"

"Let him," Grayson muttered. I punched his arm.

"I'll take care of it," Sloan said with a wicked smile. "I've got a few spells I'm itching to give a whirl."

Grayson side-eyed me as he parked the car along the edge of the road. "Should we be worried?"

"Only if she tries them out on you," I said with a smirk. "I think it's that farmhouse on the right."

"I can't believe Uncle Dave lives in a farmhouse." Nick's voice was tight with anxiety. "He's not exactly a farmer."

"But he *is* a Hunter," Sloan quipped. Nick's earnest chuckle made me flinch. This time, Grayson shot me a look that said I wasn't alone in my suspicions.

"Let's get this over with," I said, anxious to be outside.

Nick and Sloan led the way up the dirt path leading to the house while Grayson stepped close to me. He nudged my arm and then nodded at them with a raised eyebrow. His insinuation was obvious, but there was no way for me to reply meaningfully without being overheard, so I just shrugged.

We were trailing far enough behind that Nick was already knocking on the door by the time we caught up with them. Grayson was holding himself tenser than usual, almost in a fighting stance. I was contemplating mimicking him when the door flew open.

"What?" a deep voice boomed at us.

The man on the other side of the screen door bore a striking resemblance to his nephew. If I hadn't known better, I would've thought he was Nick's father.

"Dave? It's me, Nick."

"Nicky?" Dave tilted his head in confusion. "What the hell are you doing here, boy?"

"I need your help, Uncle Dave." Nick sounded strong and confident, but I could see that his hands were twitching.

Dave's eyes scanned each of us, hesitating a beat longer on Grayson. "You brought a vampire to my home?"

"Two, actually." Nick looked right at his uncle and I saw the flash of understanding in Dave's eyes.

"You are either very brave or very stupid for coming here," Dave said. "I've killed dozens of your kind. What makes you think I won't do the same to you?"

"Because you'll never get that chance." I stepped forward until I was in front of Nick. "You try to hurt either of them and you will be sorry."

Dave eyed me up and down and laughed. "And I should be scared of a pretty thing like you?"

"Try me," I said.

"What's your name, girl?"

"Isabel Jones." I kept my face impassive as Dave's registered shock. "I take it you are familiar with the Jones family?"

Dave nodded. "I went to school with your father. As far as I knew, he was never a Hunter though."

"You could say it skipped a generation. If we're done with introductions, how about letting us come inside for a chat?" I gave him my best Grayson-smile, equal parts confidence and disdain.

"I'll give you ten minutes. My wife will be home soon and she's not a fan of vampires." Dave pushed open the door, much to my surprise. I hadn't expected it to be this easy to convince him to let us inside.

We were ushered into a cozy room filled with oversized furniture. It was tidier than I had expected. Grayson had moved close behind me and took a seat so close that we were sharing a cushion on the couch. That type of behavior was so unlike him that I almost asked if something was wrong.

Sloan sat on the other side of me while Nick and Dave sat in chairs across from us.

"If I were you, I'd start talking," Dave advised, glancing at his watch.

"Have you ever heard of a vampire named Liam?" Grayson said, unable to stop himself from taking the lead.

Dave leaned back in his chair. "I've heard of him. Why?"

"He's come to Shaded Falls," Nick said before Grayson could respond. "Liam and his army have been waging a war against the supernatural locals. We're trying to figure out why so we can stop him."

"I don't know why any true vampire would want to live in the falls. Sure, the immunity from the sun is nice, but you can't exactly snack on the humans." Dave glared at Nick. "As I'm sure you've come to realize."

"That's not true anymore," Grayson said. "As of this morning, all the magic that used to protect the town has disappeared. We think maybe Liam has a witch working for him that is messing with the enchantments."

At this, Dave leaned forward. "That doesn't make sense. I can see why he'd want to unprotect the humans, but why remove the spell that protects vampires from the sun?"

"That's exactly what I'd like to know." Grayson mirrored Dave's posture, leaning forward with elbows on his knees.

"I'm sure the two spells were bound together," I said. "The whole point of the magic was to curse the town and punish the founding families by creating that dangerous balancing act. I'm sure once Liam broke the spell protecting the humans, the other spell was automatically broken as well."

"Huh. You're not just a pretty face." Dave nodded approvingly. Grayson glared at him on my behalf, a response that didn't go unnoticed. Dave looked back and forth between us. "Is the Hunter in love with a vampire?"

Before I could answer, or even decide how to answer, a voice called out, "Dave, honey, do we have company?"

Every person in the room turned toward the doorway except for Grayson, who instead straightened abruptly and his eyes widened as he turned to me.

"What's wrong?" I mouthed, putting my hand on his knee.

The flash of pain in his eyes was so sudden and so raw that it took my breath away. He turned his head slowly toward the doorway just as a pretty girl stepped into the room. She had long, dark hair with soft waves and perfect red lips that formed a wide O when she saw us. Her resemblance to Grayson was uncanny and my heart raced as I watched him stare at her. Her face was locked in an expression between a scream and a smile.

"Elsie," he said, his body shuddering from the effort of saying that one word.

I sucked in a sharp breath. The girl before us was Grayson's little sister, the very one he had almost killed when he had transitioned into a vampire.

"Grayson?" The hard edges of her face softened. "What are you doing here?"

He stood slowly, doing his best not to frighten her. She took a step back anyway and I saw the slight grimace on his face. I stood, too, badly wanting to help but knowing there was nothing I could do.

"We came to talk to Dave," Grayson said, his voice hollow and unrecognizable.

"How do you know my step-daughter?" Dave said gruffly.

Grayson flinched again, his eyes darting back and forth

between Dave and Elsie. He was processing the new revelation even as he said, "She's my sister."

"Sister?" Dave looked to Elsie for confirmation and she nodded. "Your mother said your brother was dead."

"She lied," Elsie said in a small voice.

I wanted to reach out to Grayson, to comfort him from his mother's betrayal. But I knew that would only make things worse. Grayson would never want anyone to know how much his mother's actions and words had hurt him. He hadn't even wanted to share that information with me.

"Where is she?" Grayson asked, almost sounding scared.

Elsie didn't have to answer because more footsteps were approaching the room. Instinctively, I grabbed Grayson's hand. He didn't look at me – his eyes were still locked on Elsie – but he did squeeze my hand tightly.

When Grayson's mother appeared in the doorway, I was relieved that Grayson was holding onto me. I was so close to throwing myself at her, punishing her for how badly she'd hurt her son when she abandoned him. The aching look he gave her nearly took my breath away.

"Grayson." His mother didn't sound surprised to see him there. Her green eyes were brighter than anything I'd ever seen, much like Elsie's eyes. I wondered if Grayson's eyes had been that color before he became a gold-eyed vampire.

"Mom." His voice was flat and cold. "You remarried?"

She nodded.

"Guess the wedding invitation got lost in the mail." He was masking his hurt with exaggerated sarcasm.

"It was a daytime wedding," she said with a smirk that made my blood boil. Her cold eyes dropped to where our hands were locked together. "Is she some kind of twisted human companion you use for blood?"

"Jane." Dave's voice was surprisingly harsh. "This is

Isabel Jones."

Grayson's mom stared at me. "A Jones girl? That makes you a Hunter."

"A damn good Hunter," I said, stepping slightly forward.

"That can't be true if you're holding hands with a vampire." Jane gave no indication that she was talking about her own son. "I'm not sure if anyone told you, but Hunters are actually supposed to kill vampires, not date them."

"And mothers are supposed to love their children unconditionally, not abandon them," I snapped.

"Isabel." Grayson tugged on my hand, a gentle warning.

Jane turned her attention to him. "Care to tell me what you are doing in my home, Grayson?"

"We came to speak with Dave. I had no idea you and Elsie would be here." He sounded nothing like the Grayson I was used to hearing command a vampire clan. He sounded broken. "I had no intention of violating your order that I stay away from both of you."

"This is quite the day," Dave said, sounding amused. "I find out my nephew is a vampire, my wife's son isn't actually dead, but he's also a vampire, and got to witness this delightful family reunion."

"Go to hell, Dave," Nick said, looking almost as beaten down as Grayson. "The sooner you both can get onboard with the idea that not all vampires are evil, the sooner we can resume discussing how to kill Liam."

Jane turned to Nick. "I won't be discussing anything with you."

"It's been five years," Grayson said softly.

"You almost killed Elsie," Jane said with venom dripping on her words. "You are a vampire now. What kind of mother would I be if I let you stay in this house with my daughter?"

"Mom." Elsie put her hand on Jane's arm. "I'm not scared

of Grayson."

Jane turned her glare to her daughter. "Then you are a fool. Do you not remember him ripping into your throat?"

"That was a different time," Elsie said, surprisingly looking at me instead of Grayson or her mother. "He can control it now, can't he?"

I nodded. "Yes. He's not going to hurt you."

"Just because he hasn't hurt you yet, doesn't mean he won't." Jane was unmoved by my assurances. She looked at Grayson. "Your friends can stay, but I need you to leave."

"No," Elsie said, almost yelling. "You're not sending him away. Grayson isn't going to hurt me, Mom."

"It's okay, Elsie." Grayson's shoulders dropped. "Mom is just trying to protect you. If she doesn't want me in her home, I have to respect that."

He jerked his hand away from mine so suddenly I couldn't resist. Grayson was normally very good at controlling his supernatural speed, but he was already out of the room before I could even blink. His intention was to leave me behind with Nick and Sloan, but I wasn't going to let that happen.

"Stay here," I told them. "We'll come back later."

Nick nodded, looking a little stunned by the revelations of the last few minutes. I made my way past Jane, forcing myself not to say anything rude to her. I caught up with Grayson at the car. If he had truly been anxious to get away, there was no chance I would've made it in time to stop him. But Grayson wasn't in a hurry. His hand was frozen on the door handle.

I put my hand on his back and his body jerked. He was so lost in his thoughts that he hadn't heard me approach. "Grayson." I slid my arms around him from behind. "I'm so sorry."

"It's fine." He peeled my arms away. "You should go back inside."

"No."

He turned around, no trace of any emotion on his face. "Fine. Let's just get out of here."

Grayson was completely guarded, not even glancing at me once as he drove. I had never seen him so shutdown. Even when I put my hand on his arm, he just stared straight ahead. We were in the heart of a small city and drove past a college campus. Grayson parked the car in front of a questionable looking bar.

"I need a drink," he said, exiting the car before I could respond.

A group of college guys stood in the parking lot, smoking and talking loudly in slurred speech. Grayson stomped past them without a problem, but I wasn't getting by so easily.

"Hey," the tallest one said. "Aren't you in my stats class?"

"Nope." I kept walking, my eyes trained on Grayson's back.

"Didn't you go down on Cooper at the last Sigma Chi party?" The shortest one took a step toward me. "I heard you were good. If you let me take you for a spin in the bathroom, I'll buy you a drink afterward."

My mouth was open as I was fully prepared to tell him off, but Grayson had snapped back to reality and was charging toward him.

"I will kill you," he said, twisting the guy's shirt in his hand and slamming him against a pickup truck.

"Grayson." I grabbed his arm and pulled hard. "Don't."

"This piece of shit deserves to pay for talking to you like that, Isabel." Grayson's eyes were burning like fire.

I yanked on his arm again. "Maybe so, Grayson, but you *could* kill him."

At that, he looked at me. Whatever anger had been holding his emotional wall in place dissolved and he shoved the guy away. "Just keep your damn mouth shut," he snapped at the guy who nodded furiously.

Grayson started walking away, this time slow enough for me to match his pace. We were walking with a few inches between us, but it may as well have been a mile. He stopped to hold the door open for me and I noticed that his hand was shaking, probably from the pent-up desire to hit someone.

I found us a table near the back and Grayson went to the bar to get our drinks. From the clientele, it was obvious that we were in the heart of the college campus, but it was midweek and the bar was only half full. At a few tables, tired faces were focused on thick textbooks.

"Here." Grayson slid a drink in front of me before folding his long body into the chair across from me. "Sorry about what happened outside."

"Don't be sorry," I said, glad to hear him talking again. "Just be Grayson."

"Be careful what you ask for," he said with a frown. When he raised his glass to his lip, his hand was no longer shaking.

I studied him closely, wishing for the millionth time that he wasn't so hard to decipher. I wondered if I would ever be able to understand what he was thinking and feeling, or if he would always be this infuriatingly inscrutable.

"What?" he asked wearily when he caught me staring.

"I assume you don't want to talk about what happened?" I said.

"You are correct." He took another sip of his drink.

While I wasn't surprised, I was disappointed. "I feel like I'm always going to be on the outside of your life."

"You're kidding, right?" He smirked at me. "You've

already moved into my house, Isabel, and we've been dating for less than a week."

"Inviting me into your bed isn't the same as letting me into your life." I felt pathetic even as I said the words, but it was true. "Forget it. If you don't want to talk, we don't have to talk."

"I may not be the smartest man, but I'm not dumb enough to let this drop." He set his glass on the table and leaned forward. "What do you want from me? Do you want me to pour out my heart to you? Do you want me to cry?"

"I said forget it." I was seeing a new side of Grayson and it wasn't one that I enjoyed. "I get that you're hurting, but you don't have to be a jerk to me."

Predicting that he would say something else cold and aloof, I stood up. "I'm going to the ladies' room. Maybe work on adjusting your attitude while I'm gone?"

"I'll get right on that," he muttered.

I spent what felt like ten minutes washing my hands and staring blankly at my reflection in the mirror. I hadn't expected Grayson to pour his heart out to me, but his angry demeanor was unexpected. Grayson and I had only known each other for a few weeks and we'd only been dating for a few days. Maybe the Grayson I was seeing now was the real Grayson. That would line up with the Grayson I saw in the vampire council meetings.

When I finally headed back to the table, I was confused to see it was empty. Our glasses were still there, but Grayson was gone. I scanned the bar quickly and spotted his broad shoulders hunched over a jukebox. He punched a button and the room filled with music. He turned and spotted me across the room.

My heart did a familiar flip and I could feel the magnetic change between us. Even when I was annoyed with Grayson,

I still adored him. As if he could read my mind, he headed in my direction with a faint smile on his face.

"I know you're mad at me, but will you just ignore that for a few minutes and dance with me?" He held out his hand and raised a hopeful eyebrow.

I wasn't ready to forgive him yet, but selfishly I wanted to be in his arms. "Okay," I said, putting my hand in his. "Let's dance."

Unlike Mack's, every person in the bar was watching us as Grayson moved to the center of the room. He found a semi-open spot on the floor and pulled me close. I let out the breath I was holding as his arms went around me.

"I wasn't sure if you'd say yes," he admitted.

I circled my arms around his neck and kept my eyes focused at a point over his shoulder. "I don't like fighting with you."

"But we're so good at it," he said with a laugh.

"Everyone is staring at us," I said, changing the subject to something safer. "I don't think this bar usually has a lot of slow-dancing."

"I don't think these people are used to seeing someone as beautiful as you," he said softly. I lifted my gaze to look into his eyes and was rewarded with a smile. "When I was growing up, my parents used to dance like this in the kitchen when they thought Elsie and I weren't paying attention."

Revealing that memory was Grayson's way of apologizing. He was telling me something very private about his family and also proving that he had, in fact, very much let me into his life. "Your childhood sounds disgustingly sweet," I said, the ice around my heart completely melted. "And this explains your romantic tendencies."

"I've asked you to dance twice, Isabel. I'd hardly say that makes me a romantic." He looked away, embarrassed.

"You've done a lot more than that." I moved one hand from his neck, down to his chest. When he turned back to me, I said, "You met me at school every day for a month, even when I told you I wasn't interested. I didn't realize it at the time, but you weren't doing that to keep any eye on me. You were there because you wanted to be with me."

"You really just figured that out?" he said with a laugh. "Isabel, if it was up to me, we would never be apart."

I moved closer, resting my head in the soft curve of his neck. "You don't have to talk about your mother, but I want you to know that everything she said about you is wrong. You are a good man and I fall more in love with you every single day."

His arms tightened around me and I could've sworn that his heart skipped a beat beneath my hand, even though that shouldn't be possible. "You are the best thing that has ever happened to me."

We weren't even moving to the music any longer. Grayson was holding me so close that I almost couldn't breathe, but dying in his arms seemed like the best possible way to go.

"The music has stopped," I said, my lips moving softly over his skin.

"Is that a problem?" One of his hands moved to the back of my neck and he tugged at my hair gently until I lifted my head. "Do you want me to let go of you?"

I immediately shook my head. "No. Never."

"Glad we're in agreement on that." He brought his lips to mine, grazing softly as he said, "I'm yours, Isabel Jones. Completely."

Mine, I thought as he kissed me harder. *Grayson Parker, vampire overlord and drop-dead gorgeous man, was all mine.*

14

I was so swept away by Grayson's kiss, by the tingles running through my body, that I completely forgot we were in the middle of a bar. Grayson had a way of making me forget everything that wasn't him.

"We have to go back eventually," I said when I finally pulled away for air. "We left Sloan and Nick behind."

"I guess we do need to go back for Sloan," he said, conveniently not adding Nick's name. "But I think we can stay here a little longer."

"You never finished your drink," I reminded him.

He smiled faintly as he traced two fingers along my jaw. "Darling, kissing you is far more intoxicating than any alcohol."

"I can't believe we've only been doing this for a week," I said.

"I've been in love with you a lot longer than that." Grayson looked as though he was about to kiss me again, but then thought better of it. "We should head back and check on the others."

He was right, of course, but that didn't make it any easier

to step away from him. That struggle manifested itself in a painful grimace that made Grayson laugh.

"This would be so much easier if you were hideous and cruel," I said with a slow shake of my head.

"Well, you could always go back to Nick if that's what you're interested in," Grayson said a little too seriously.

"Ha. Ha." Before I could tease him for being jealous, my phone vibrated in my pocket. I glanced at it and frowned. "Speaking of the ex, Nick says they are done."

Grayson's jaw clenched, but he didn't comment. He might not like that my ex-boyfriend still texted me, but it was a necessary evil. The drive back to the house was quiet, but not nearly as tense as our drive to the bar. Grayson wasn't exactly relaxed, but he also didn't look like he was in pain anymore.

"Think Dave and Jane were helpful?" I was hesitant to mention his mom, but it wasn't a topic we could avoid forever.

"No clue. I'm surprised Mom even let Nick stay in the house. Guess she only hates vampires that she gave birth to." His hands tightened on the steering wheel.

"Elsie looks just like you," I said cautiously. "Except for the eyes, obviously."

He laughed a little. "We used to have that in common, too. I'm not sure she'd want to be associated with me now, though."

"Don't be too sure of that, Grayson. She wasn't scared of you." I remembered how Elsie had stood up to her mother. That couldn't have been easy for her.

"Well, Elsie never was a genius." Grayson stared glumly straight ahead. "Look, even if Elsie isn't scared of me, I'm not going to pull her into my darkness. It's bad enough that I've done that to you."

"You didn't do anything to me," I said. "This is my choice."

The glow from the car's interior lights cast an odd glow over Grayson's face, turning his skin a shade of pale blue that only made him look even more ethereal. "I never thought I would say this, but I can't wait to get back to Shaded Falls."

"Missing Dorian?" I teased.

Grayson glanced at me, a small laugh escaping despite his attempt to hold it back. "Funny, Jones, but no."

"I'm sure he's missing you. I think Dorian is used to getting a naked-Grayson fix every night now." I added with a leer, "So am I."

"We're about to walk back into a house with my mom, sister, and your ex-boyfriend. Keep your mind out of the gutter." Even as he scolded me, he reached over and squeezed my thigh very suggestively. "If we move efficiently, we can be back at the mansion in just a few hours."

"Aren't we supposed to be trying to save the supernatural world?" I asked extra-sweetly. "That will be a little hard to do from your bed."

"We won't know until we try," he said with a grin, looking much more like his usual self. He barely seemed to notice that we were already back at the house.

I nudged his hand away. "Later, Parker. Stay focused."

"Think we can just tell Nick and Sloan we're here, or do we have to go inside?" Grayson asked, his emotional wall slowly sliding into place.

"I think you should at least say goodbye to Elsie," I said gently.

Grayson sighed. "You're right."

We walked toward the house slowly and I assumed that Grayson was just nervous about seeing Jane again. But then he put his hand on my arm. "Something is wrong," he said quietly.

"Wrong?" I saw that he was scanning the open farm field. His eyes darted suddenly to the house, narrowing as he listened closer.

"We have company," he said. The next word he mouthed without making a sound. *Liam.*

In the few seconds it took me to process what was happening, Grayson's hand closed like a vice over my arm and he yanked me toward the farmhouse. He slammed open the front door and shoved me inside before locking it behind us.

"A locked door isn't going to keep him out," I said, but Grayson was already headed to the living room where we found the others still engaged in deep conversation.

Nick caught the frantic look on my face and said, "What's wrong, Iz?"

"Liam," I said, still watching Grayson. He disappeared from the room without an explanation.

"Liam?" Nick was on his feet, but he froze in the middle of the room. He must have heard or sensed whatever had caused Grayson's frenzy, because he swore under his breath.

Grayson returned with a stack of kitchen knives. "These aren't ideal weapons, but they will have to do unless you've got a secret arsenal of weapons around here."

"What's happening?" Sloan asked. She came and stood next to Nick. "Is Liam here?"

"He's out there," Grayson said, nodding in the general direction of outside as he handed me one of the knives. "With an army from what I can tell."

"A few kitchen knives aren't going to stop him," Nick said, but he took one from Grayson regardless.

I looked at my knife and then looked at Sloan and Jane.

"Maybe we don't need the knives. We've got two witches in our arsenal."

Grayson looked at me in surprise and nodded slowly. "Good call."

"Can you do something? A protection spell or whatever?" I asked Sloan. I was still too annoyed at Jane to address her directly.

"Yeah, I can probably do that." Sloan glanced at Jane. "I could use your help, though."

"Follow me," Jane said curtly, heading through a doorway that lead to the dining room. As she and Sloan started lighting candles on the table, Grayson and Nick peered out the window.

"You know how to use that?" Dave said, gesturing to my knife.

"You mean for more than chopping vegetables?" I said. "Don't worry about me."

Dave scoffed. "I'm not worried about *you*, girl. I'm worried about how a pretty, young thing like you is going to help save my ass."

Grayson turned from the window, prepared to shut Dave down with some harsh words, but I beat him to it. "No need to worry – I'm not going to."

Dave narrowed his eyes at me and Grayson chuckled. "I'd advise you to stay out of her way. She's far more than just a pretty face," he said. Humor danced in Grayson's eyes as he winked at me and I was struck at how easily he'd been able to ignore that we were about to be attacked. I rewarded him with a forced smile.

"How much time do we have?" I asked.

Nick answered without turning away from the window. "Liam is positioning his army. They'll attack soon."

"Sloan? How's it coming in there?" I turned the knife in my hand, wishing it was just a little heftier.

"We're ready." Sloan sounded calmer than anyone else in the house. "But we need to be able to concentrate."

I turned to Grayson. "We need to take the fight outside."

"Outside?" He was unconvinced. "We'll be completely exposed out there."

"We'll be trapped in here." I stepped closer to him and lowered my voice. "If we let them inside, we'll be leading them right to Elsie."

Grayson looked past me, his eyes landing on his sister. She had been so quiet, curled up in a chair and watching everything with wide eyes, that all of us had forgotten she was there. The rest of us were anxious, but we weren't helpless like Elsie.

"What should we do with her?" Grayson asked.

I was stunned. This wasn't the type of thing that Grayson ever needed my opinion on. He never hesitated to make decisions in battle. But then again, he'd never had to worry about his family while making those decisions.

"Elsie," I turned to her, trying to look confident. "Go into the dining room and get under the table. Don't come out until Grayson or I come get you."

She looked frightened, but she stood and nodded. "Okay."

"Wait." I went to her and held out my knife. "Take this. If anyone tries to get you that isn't one of the people in this house right now, don't hesitate to use it."

"Okay," she repeated, looking at me with those dazzling green eyes. Elsie looked so scared, and looked so much like Grayson, that I couldn't stop myself from giving her a quick hug.

"It's going to be okay," I told her.

Grayson waited until she was safely hidden under the table before saying, "You can't go outside unprotected, Isabel."

"I'm not unprotected." I held up my hand. "This is far more deadly than that knife."

"Right." He looked skeptical, but we didn't have time to debate it. It was time to fight. Grayson was close enough to touch me, but he refrained. With a meaningful look, he said, "Be careful."

"Stay close to me," I said with a playful smile. "I'll protect you."

"I have no doubt you will," he said. His eyes darted back to the window and I knew that it was time for us to make our move.

It was cold outside. Somehow, I hadn't noticed the chill earlier, but now it was undeniable. My breath fogged the air in front of me, but it didn't prevent me from seeing the row of dark shadows moving in our direction.

"Nick and Dave are guarding the back of the house," Grayson said. He was close enough that his arm was touching mine. His presence was always a comfort, even if we were facing an army of vampires that wanted to kill us. In a voice that was almost inaudible, he said, "Liam wants you alive, Isabel. He will kill me to get to you, but he has no intention of harming you. Remember that."

I knew that Grayson was trying to tell me something important, but my brain wasn't able to decipher the code. I was still running the probabilities through my head of the four of us fighting against at least twenty enemy vampires. The odds were most definitely not in our favor.

This time, there was no casual banter before the attack. One moment, the army was moving slowly toward us. The next moment, a vampire was right in front of me. Grayson was able to react with supernatural speed and kicked him hard in the chest, sending him flying back several feet. I was grateful for the extra seconds he had given me to prepare for the next attack.

When the next vampire lunged at me, I was ready. I dropped and swept my leg, bringing the vampire to the ground. Then I shoved my hand hard against its chest and as it snapped its fangs at me, a familiar heat radiated over my skin. It snarled as a soft glow emanated from my hand, straight into its heart.

The entire kill took less than 15 seconds. I followed it quickly with three more kills and whirled to take out a fifth vampire, but I stopped short when I realized the vampire I was about to touch was Liam.

"Incredible," he breathed, staring at the decomposing bodies around us. His gaze lingered on my hand for a long time before moving to my face. "I *must* have you, Isabel. A power like yours combined with my strength would make us indestructible."

"Why don't you come a little closer so I can touch you?" I said with a feigned smile. "I promise, it will hurt so good."

Liam lifted his lip in a snarl. "Let's make a deal. You let me taste you first, and then I'll let you touch me."

"Careful, Liam. I might start to think you are obsessed with me, or my blood at least." I remembered what Grayson had said. Liam wanted me alive because he wanted my blood. If I was dead, he couldn't feed off me. "What is it about my blood that enthralls you enough to cause you to start a war?"

"You really don't know?" He smiled in delight. "Your boyfriend must be scared to tell you. Once you know the truth, it's doubtful you'll trust him ever again."

I glanced quickly to my left and saw Grayson finish off a

vampire before starting in our direction. We only had a few seconds before he would close the distance between us.

"What is it about my blood?" I said.

"You are not pure Hunter, Isabel," Liam said. He grabbed my arm and pulled me closer and I made no attempt to stop him. "Your father descended from a Hunter lineage, but your mother was a witch. That makes you a rare hybrid and your blood is even more exceptional."

"What happens if you drink it?" My hand twitched at my side, ready to burn Liam the second it became necessary.

Liam's head dropped, his face just inches from my own. "That is what I'd like to find out. If I had to guess, I believe that your magical powers are transferable because of your Hunter blood."

Now, I understood why Liam wanted my blood. A vampire couldn't steal magic by drinking from witches. Their power was transferred by genetics, not by bloodsharing. But my blood wasn't pure and the Hunter blood inside me changed everything, or at least that was Liam's hypothesis.

"That sounds like nothing more than wishful thinking to me." I wanted to look for Grayson, but there was no way to do that without Liam noticing. If I could just stall him a few seconds longer, we might be able to catch him by surprise. "You're already a vampire. Do you really need magical blood, too?"

"Vampires are still able to be killed, love." Liam used that pet name too easily for my liking. "Like if I let you touch my chest right now, you could kill me. But if I had magical blood, I would be virtually immortal."

Grayson had yet to make an appearance and I was tired of being so close to Liam while he was leering at me so unabashedly.

"I'm never going to willingly let you drink from me," I said, yanking my arm away from him. "If you want my blood, you'll have to kill me to get it."

"There are ways I can convince you without killing you," he said with a wicked grin. Liam threw his arm out to the side and caught Nick's arm. He squeezed it hard until Nick's hand opened and the knife fell to the ground. Then he jerked his arm and brought Nick close, circling his arm around Nick's neck. "How about we make a trade? Some of your blood in exchange for your friend's life."

Grayson had finally reached us, but he froze when I gave him a warning look. "All of this," I said, waving my arms through the air, "is because you want my blood?"

"Just a little of your blood," Liam said, tightening his grip on Nick. Just one twist of his arm and he would tear Nick's head from his body.

I noticed that Nick's knife had fallen at my feet. There was no way I could grab it and make a move on Liam fast enough, but I did have one move left. I swooped down and snatched the knife.

"Isabel, love. Do you really think that's going to help?" Liam was grinning at me, not at all worried that I might kill him. "You'll never be able to kill me before I kill him."

"Maybe not," I agreed. "But I could kill myself."

Orange flames danced in Liam's eyes. "You wouldn't!"

"Let him go or you'll find out just how serious I am." I ran the edge of the blade over the palm of my hand.

"Isabel." The urgency in Grayson's tone almost made me back down.

"Let him go," I repeated, looking only at Liam. "Or you'll never have a chance to taste my blood."

Liam's nostrils flared as he appraised me. "Nice try,

Hunter, but we both know you'll never sacrifice yourself to save a vampire."

At this, I looked at Nick. He was a vampire, true, but he was so much more than that. He was the first person I'd loved after losing everything. He was the first person that had truly loved me, besides my parents. Nick was the guy who had sacrificed his own life to save me. He was my friend and part of my heart still belonged to him. Then I looked at Grayson, the man that had claimed the rest of my heart. His eyes were pleading me not to follow through on my threat.

"You don't know anything about me," I said to Liam. Without any hesitation, I thrust the knife into my side.

The pain was debilitating, bringing me to my knees. Grayson let out a terrified yell and started toward me. Liam was faster. He threw Nick away with a loud growl and dove at me, catching me before I hit the ground.

"You stupid girl," he said, pushing his hand to the open wound. The smell of blood was overwhelming, even to me. Liam's face contorted as his fangs protruded menacingly. He was completely overtaken by the demon within and just as his fangs were about to sink into my neck, I slammed my palm hard against his chest.

The heat was sudden and tremendous. His head jerked back in surprise and Grayson and Nick stopped just before grabbing Liam. I bit hard on the insides of my cheeks to keep the pain in my side from overwhelming me and breaking my focus. Liam's fangs retreated and his eyes turned a shocking shade of blue just before the life flashed out of them completely.

Nick threw his lifeless body away and Grayson caught me before I toppled over, overcome by pain and dizziness.

"What the hell were you thinking?" Grayson said,

pushing his hand hard against my side. Blood oozed between his fingers.

"I had to," was all I could say.

"We need to get her into the house," Nick said. I noted the pained expression on his face and that he was keeping his distance from me. *The blood,* I realized. It must be almost impossible for him to resist.

Grayson scooped me into his arms and headed toward the house. I could see the rest of Liam's vampires moving toward us, but they stopped abruptly. Jane and Sloan must have gotten a protective barrier in place. I relaxed a little and closed my eyes.

"Isabel, no. Stay with me." Grayson gave me a slight squeeze.

"I'm not going anywhere," I said, burrowing closer to him. I was suddenly very cold and very tired. "I just need to rest."

"Please, Isabel. Don't leave me."

I wanted to tell him not to worry, that I would never leave him. I wanted to tell him that everything was going to be fine, that my plan had worked. We had killed Liam and I had saved Nick. We were safe inside the house with two powerful witches protecting us. I wanted to tell him all those things and look into his beautiful eyes while I did that, but I couldn't. The exhaustion was too heavy and too consuming. With a last shaking breath, darkness fell.

15

I didn't recognize the room I was in. The bedspread was pink and the walls were covered in floral wallpaper. My entire body ached as I struggled into a sitting position. Grayson was asleep next to me, looking far too pale. I reached over to touch his cheek, but a quiet voice stopped me.

"He just fell asleep a few minutes ago. You should let him rest."

It was Elsie. She was watching me from the doorway with a mixture of relief and curiosity. "How long have I been out?" I said, my voice cracking several times.

"Just over a day. Grayson stayed awake as long as he could, but you know the effect that the sun has on vampires." Elsie came closer to the bed and picked up a glass of water from the bedside table. She handed it to me and then perched against the windowsill. "We thought you were going to die."

"So did I," I said grimly, putting a hand over the heavy bandage wrapped around my torso. "How bad is the damage?"

"Pretty bad," Elsie said bluntly. "You lost a lot of blood and had internal damage. If Grayson hadn't given you his blood, you would've died."

My eyes widened. "I was cured by vampire blood?"

"And some magical herbs. Mom's a big believe in using nature to enhance the body's healing properties." Elsie smiled for the first time. "She's not completely crazy, I swear."

"This is your room?" I guessed.

"I thought you'd be more comfortable in here than on the couch downstairs." She glanced briefly at Grayson. "Plus, the whole privacy factor."

I realized that I was no longer wearing my own clothes. "Is this yours, also?" I asked, gesturing to the nightshirt covered in vibrant rainbows.

"Grayson asked for something that wouldn't irritate your wound. Sorry, it's kind of lame." Elsie was looking at her brother again. "I've never seen him so worried."

"He's good at worrying," I said softly.

"He loves you so much," she continued. "Even when you were bleeding all over, he never hesitated. I don't know many vampires that could resist the urge to feed like that, but it never even crossed his mind. All he could think about was saving your life."

A wave of emotion bubbled in my chest and I took a deep breath. "I know what he did to you, Elsie, but you have to know that he never wanted to hurt you. He would rather die than hurt any human, but especial someone he loves."

"Like you," she said, turning back to me with a smile as Grayson began to stir. "I should go. You both need to rest."

"Thank you for everything," I said, gesturing to the room and the nightshirt.

"Don't mention it." Elsie was already across the room

and she tossed a small wave before closing the door behind her.

With no one to stop me, I stroked Grayson's cheek with two fingers. His dark eyelashes fluttered and his lips parted. "Isabel?"

"It's me, sweetheart." I smiled as his eyes flew open.

He bolted straight up, his hand cupping my cheek. "You're awake."

"I am," I said, my smile growing. "Thanks to you."

Grayson closed his eyes and touched his forehead gently against mine. "I thought I was going to lose you, Isabel."

"You didn't lose me," I said, putting a hand to his chest. "I'm right here."

"I don't know what I would have done if I'd lost you," he said. "If my blood hadn't worked..."

"But it did. It worked." I ran my hand up to the back of his neck, curving my fingers into his dark waves. My lips brushed lightly over his. "You saved me, Grayson."

He pressed his lips tentatively to mine, like he was kissing me for the first time. I wanted more, but he resisted. "You're still recovering," he said, forcing a weak smile as he pulled back. "Let's not get carried away."

"I'm fine," I insisted, but Grayson had already moved away.

"You might be, but I'm not." He glanced at the window. The curtains were pulled, but soft sunlight trickled through the dense fabric.

It was clear that Grayson's energy was sapped. "Of course, I'm sorry." I settled back against my pillow. "Get some rest, sweetheart."

He surprised me by moving closer, draping his arm around me as he lay his head on my chest. "I just need to feel your heart beating," he said.

I wrapped my arms around him, stroking my fingers gently through his hair. This was the most vulnerable Grayson had ever been with me and I felt tears pooling in my eyes. "Every beat is yours," I said.

"I cherish each one more than you could ever know." His voice was heavy with sleep. Within seconds, he was asleep again and just a short time after that, I joined him.

The next time I woke up, I was alone. Only a faint light was visible beyond the curtains and I suspected it was sunset. Grayson's energy would've recharged by now and I could feel some of my own strength returning as well. I was anxious to leave Elsie's bedroom, but I wasn't eager to parade around in the skimpy nightshirt. After climbing slowly to my feet, I noticed a t-shirt and pair of sweatpants on the dresser.

With a great effort, I managed to pull the nightshirt over my head. I was naked, except for the white bandage wrapped around my stomach. I thought about peeling back the layers to check out the damage, but I was worried about reopening the wound. Instead, I reached for the sweatpants. It took a few minutes to get dressed, and I had to rest afterward, but eventually I opened the door.

After a short walk down a quiet hallway, I paused at the top of the stairs. My side was aching, but it was tolerable. I wasn't sure how it would feel after descending 15 steps, but I didn't have much of a choice. I took it slow, pausing after each step. When I was nearly at the bottom, Grayson appeared.

"Why didn't you call out to me?" he demanded, eyes full of concern. "I would've helped you."

"I can walk just fine on my own, Grayson," I said, holding back a wince as I took the last step. "I'm not an invalid."

"Actually," Sloan said, grinning over Grayson's shoulder, "that's exactly what you are."

"Aren't you supposed to be my friend?" I said. Grayson hovered protectively next to me and I took his arm to make him feel useful. "Talk about kicking someone when they are down."

Sloan rolled her eyes. "Stop feeling sorry for yourself. You aren't dead and you've got a hot boyfriend to nurse you back to health. What more could you want?"

Grayson cleared his throat. "Mom is making dinner. Are you hungry?"

"Starved," I said instantly. Then I felt guilty because Grayson was probably also hungry and he had no available blood source. "Where's Nick?"

"He's out back with Dave chopping firewood." Grayson grimaced. "Elsie is offering them emotional support."

"What does that mean?" I said.

Sloan giggled. "Elsie has a little crush on our Nicholas."

"Really?" I laughed, too. "She could do worse."

"She could do a lot better," Grayson said. "Let's go outside and get some fresh air."

"And keep an eye on Elsie?" I teased.

Grayson narrowed his eyes and frowned. "I know that you think you are cute, but... okay, fine you are. However, you'd be cuter if you were supporting me instead of mocking my distress."

"You're right." I forced away the smile and nodded. "No more mocking. This news is obviously very disturbing."

"Whatever, Jones." He tried to glare at me, but instead I received an involuntary smile that made my heart flutter. "Why do you have to be so damn cute?"

"You two are disgusting." Sloan waved her arm wildly. "Please leave before I puke."

Grayson put his arm across my shoulders and I leaned into him. Just being close to him erased some of the pain in my side. He led me outside and helped me into a chair. I stared at the pink and orange streaks in the sky as Grayson pulled a chair next to mine and took my hand.

"It's a beautiful sunset," I said. Several yards away, near a pile of logs, Dave and Nick were taking turns with an axe. Elsie sat nearby on an old tree stump, staring adoringly at Nick who was completely oblivious.

"Are you cold?" Grayson asked nervously.

The air was a little chilly, but it had been too warm inside the house. "No, it feels good."

"Are you sure?" He looked ready to spring from his seat.

"Grayson, relax. I'm fine." I squeezed his hand. "I'm not a delicate flower."

"You almost died," he said quietly. "To save him."

His words were so unexpected, they took my breath away. Of all the things he might have said, I had never expected him to be angry that I'd made my choice to protect Nick. "Grayson, I did that to save everyone. Did you expect me to just let Liam kill Nick?"

"He doesn't deserve your love." Grayson was glaring at Nick. "He has said so many terrible things about you."

"So he deserved to die?" I asked indignantly. "Be serious, Grayson. Nick hasn't been perfect, but neither have I. If the situation was reversed, I guarantee you that Nick would have sacrificed himself to save me."

Grayson was quiet for a long moment. I continued to study his face, desperate to understand the haunted look in his eyes. "I don't know if I'll ever be okay with Rockson. I hate how he has treated you and how you almost died because of him. I hate that he won your heart before I did. But most of all, I hate that you still love him."

"Grayson–"

"I saw it in your eyes, Isabel." He turned to me. "When

E.J. KING

Liam was threatening to kill Nick, I saw the anguish in your eyes."

"I do love Nick. But you already knew that." I searched his eyes. "You know that how I feel about Nick is nothing like what I feel for you, right?" The slight narrowing of his eyes said that he wasn't sure. "I love you so deeply that sometimes I forget I ever had a life before I met you. When I'm not with you, all I can think about is how amazing it will feel when I'm with you again. My heart skips a beat every time you smile at me. I don't just love you, Grayson Parker. I adore you with every fiber of my being. Please tell me you know that."

"I do now," he said, putting his lips to the back of my hand. "You can't ever do that to me again, Isabel. If you had died... I'm not interested in my life without you in it."

I leaned over, kissed his cheek, and said, "I'm not going anywhere. You are stuck with me, Parker."

"Sorry, I didn't mean to interrupt." Jane had appeared in front of us and from the way Grayson flinched, I could tell I wasn't the only one surprised to see her. "Dinner is ready."

"Thanks," I said, recovering first. "I appreciate you going to the trouble."

"It's no trouble." Her eyes danced back and forth between us. "You look much better today, Isabel."

"Almost good as new," I said. "Thanks to Grayson."

She frowned slightly as she looked at her son. "Grayson, I'm very sorry for the way I reacted when I first saw you in my house."

"It's fine." Grayson's hand tightened around mine.

"It's not, but you must understand that the last time I saw you, Elsie almost died." Jane swallowed and looked away. "Over the last five years, I've learned everything I can about the supernatural world. In all my research, I never came across any stories of vampires living peacefully alongside

180

humans. It wasn't until I saw the two of you together that I even realized it might be possible and even then, I wasn't sure if the affection was genuine."

Jane's face twisted and I understood why. She had thought that I was somehow under Grayson's compulsion, that he had just been using me as a walking blood bag. "What was it that convinced you?" I asked.

"Last night, you were bleeding so much that Nick had to leave the house just to get away. But Grayson stayed with you. He never even came close to feeding on you." Jane looked only at me and I felt Grayson shifting in his chair. This entire conversation was making him uncomfortable. "There was no denying his concern for you and his determination to keep you alive. There is no denying that he loves you."

"There's no denying that he loves you and Elsie, also," I said, still not ready to forgive her for the way she had treated Grayson.

She gave me a long look and nodded slowly. "I'm not a perfect woman, but I did what I thought I had to do to protect my daughter. Grayson, I'm sorry that I had to leave you, but I'm not sorry for taking Elsie away."

"I understand," Grayson said, sounding as if he actually meant the words. "I've never blamed you for your decision to leave."

"I've blamed myself every day," Jane said, her voice cracking with just a hint of emotion as she looked at her son. "I'm glad that you found Isabel. You deserve to have love in your life, Grayson, even if I haven't shown you that for the last five years."

The others had started toward the house with their arms full of firewood. Jane blinked a few times and tested a smile. "Dinner is ready whenever you want to come inside."

"Thank you," I said, giving her a genuine smile. "We'll be right in."

She nodded and headed inside with the others close behind her. Nick broke away, much to Elsie's disappointment, and approached us hesitantly. "You look good, Iz. You really had us worried."

"I'm alright, Nick." I pulled my hand away from Grayson's and used both hands to push myself out of the chair. Grayson jumped to his feet, prepared to help me, but I gave him a firm shake of my head. "Relax, boyfriend. I've got this."

Nick smirked. "Glad to see she wasn't stubbornly independent with just me."

"Hey!" I glared at Nick. "I just saved your life. The least you could do is not talk shit about me right in front of me."

"He's not wrong," Grayson grumbled.

"Really? Now you're ganging up on me?" I put a hand on my side as I straightened. Ever muscle screamed in protest. "I liked it better when you just glared at each other while exuding toxic masculinity."

"I'm sure we'll be back there in no time," Nick said with a chuckle. "Especially since I'm about to ask if I can have a moment alone with you."

Grayson surprised us both by laughing. "Just try not to almost get yourself killed this time, Rockson."

He grazed a hand lightly over my back as he walked behind me, heading inside without a backward glance.

"What's wrong with him?" Nick asked, looking befuddled. "He didn't even glare at me or ball his hand into a fist."

"Maybe because you didn't say anything rude to me this time," I said pointedly.

He ducked his head, properly chagrined. "That's actually what I wanted to talk to you about. I know I've been a giant ass lately, especially to you, and I'm really sorry. This vampire transition has been hard and it's bringing out my worst tendencies. That's not an excuse, that's just me acknowledging that I've been a total jerk. I'm still not thrilled about you and Gray, but I'm glad you found someone who treats you right. It's clear that he loves you and I'm pretty sure you feel the same about him."

"I do," I said quickly.

"Good. You deserve to be happy, Iz." Nick smiled. "I also promise not to walk in on the two of you ever again."

"Thanks." My cheeks flushed. "I'm sure Grayson will appreciate that when I tell him."

"I'm sure he's been listening this whole time." Nick's face screwed into a grimace as he heard Grayson respond with words that my human ears couldn't hear. "Your boyfriend is quite the charmer."

"No argument from me," I said.

Nick frowned. "We better go inside. The humans are tired of waiting for us and your vampire is worried about you."

"Ugh, I'm fine, Grayson," I said, rolling my eyes as I headed toward the door.

We all sat down to eat together at the dinner table. Jane had gone overboard, preparing steaks for each of us. The boys were served theirs extra-rare and I tried to ignore the red liquid that was left behind on their plates. Surprisingly, it was a civil meal and after I helped Jane with the dishes, it was time to go home.

"Will you come back soon?" Elsie asked Grayson at the door. We all noticed her quick glance at Nick.

"I'll come back," Grayson promised her. "Probably alone."

"You have to bring Isabel," she insisted, not understanding the true meaning of his comment.

Grayson nodded. "Sure. I'll do that."

After Elsie hugged Grayson, she threw her arms around me and said, "Take care of him, okay? He needs someone to make him laugh and have fun."

"I'll do my best," I promised.

As we walked to the car, Grayson put his arm around me. This time, it wasn't an attempt to help me, it was a genuine expression of affection. I leaned into him and he dropped a kiss on top of my head. "Are you sure you're up for the car ride?"

I nodded. "Let's go home."

16

Shaded Falls was exactly the way we had left it. Over the next four weeks, the magic remained ineffective and the vampires were banished from the daylight. Sloan and I returned to school and tried to carry on normal lives. With Liam dead, the primary threat to the town had been eliminated, but Jim had decided not to return to the falls yet. Sadie was still recovering and needed a little more time.

I stayed at the mansion most nights, but occasionally I retreated to Jim's house for some privacy or crashed with Sloan when her parents were out of town. I'd fully recovered from my injury after about a week, but Grayson was still in over-protective mode. He wouldn't train with me and at night he wouldn't touch me, no matter how much I tried to tempt him.

"Still nothing?" Sloan asked me as we drove from the school to the mansion. We'd just finished our last Friday classes and I was complaining about Grayson's newly-found celibacy. "He's not hiding a performance issue, is he?"

"I don't think vampires have that problem," I said.

"Maybe you need to invest in some scandalous lingerie," she suggested.

I sighed. "Last night, I tried complete nudity and he just threw a blanket over me."

"I hate to say this, but I think you need to talk to him about it. He's clearly got some kind of mental block about getting freaky with you." Sloan's eyes darted nervously between me and the road.

"I know. Communication. It's just that this was the one thing we never had to discuss. It just worked with us." I didn't say out loud what I had been worrying about for the last month. I was afraid that Grayson might not be attracted to me anymore.

"I'm sure it's nothing," Sloan said quickly. "He still completely smitten with you. Any girl would kill to have a guy look at her the way that Grayson looks at you."

My eyes narrowed. "Speaking of other girls, I haven't heard you talk about a guy of your own in ages. What's the deal?"

"There is no deal." She became very busy with changing the radio station.

"You're seeing someone!" I slapped her arm. "Tell me everything."

Sloan pressed her lips together and stared straight ahead. After a full minute of me begging her for details, she finally said, "You're not going to like it."

"Please tell me it isn't Dorian," I said with a groan.

"It's not Dorian, but it is someone with whom you have a complicated past." She parked the car on the street in front of the mansion.

It hit me in a sudden rush. "Nick?"

She nodded, still not looking at me. "I'm sorry, Izzy. I know it's girl code not to date your friend's ex and I never meant for it to happen, but we've been spending so much time together at the mansion and he's been really nice to me, helping me practice my magic, and you can't deny that he *is* very hot and–"

"Sloan, breathe." I couldn't tell what exactly my feeling was about Sloan dating Nick, but it wasn't anger. "If you two like each other, don't let me get in the way."

"You don't care?" she asked hopefully, turning toward me.

"I've been with Grayson for two months, Sloan. That's twice the amount of time I dated Nick. I'm definitely over him." I smirked. "We're so over each other, we don't even hate each other anymore."

"Nick never hated you," she said quietly.

I nodded. "I know. I never hated him either. I want him to be happy, even if that means he dates my best friend."

"We aren't officially dating," Sloan said quickly. "We just kissed, once. I told Nick I wanted to talk to you before it went any further."

"I appreciate that, but it's really okay. You have my blessing." I grinned. "But let's not go on a double date, okay?"

"Deal," she said with a loud laugh.

"Not to pry, but what about Beth?" I asked. Despite Sloan's best efforts, we hadn't been able to track Beth and Jeremy after Liam's death. She suspected they were being hidden by a protective spell and the only way to find them would be to find the witch that was hiding them.

"She and Nick weren't dating or anything. They just hooked up a few times." Sloan frowned. "Nick swears it was nothing serious and I'm choosing to believe him."

"I'm sure he's telling the truth," I said, forcing an encouraging smile. "You should give him a chance."

It was still daylight outside, but it was a cloudy day and I was hoping that Grayson would be up earlier than usual. Most days, we only had a few hours in the evening to spend time together. We usually just hung out at the mansion, but at least one night per week, Grayson insisted on taking me out on a date.

Sloan and I parted ways inside the mansion. I assumed she was meeting up with Nick, but I didn't ask. It was one thing for them to date, but it was another thing for me to know too many details about it. I followed the familiar path to Grayson's bedroom and opened the door slowly.

Grayson was still asleep, so I entered quietly and dropped my bag in one of the leather chairs. I tossed my jacket on top of the bag and kicked off my shoes before creeping over to the bed. Grayson looked so peaceful in his sleep that I hated to wake him up, but his leg shifted and his eyes fluttered which meant he would be awake soon anyway.

I crawled onto the bed and moved over him, lowering my body slowly. "Grayson?" I said in a whisper.

His arm swooped around me at the same time that his eyes opened. "This is the only way I ever want to wake up." His lips curled into a perfect smile and I pressed my lips over his. His arm tightened around me until my body was pressed against every inch of his body.

His kisses were eager, his hands relentless, and his body completely responsive to my touch. Grayson was as turned on by me as I was by him, but when my fingers skimmed over the button of his pants, he closed a hand around my wrist.

"What's wrong?" I asked breathlessly.

"Nothing, darling." He kissed my neck.

I pushed him away and sat up, resting on my heels. I was still straddling Grayson and there was no denying that he wanted me, but he closed his eyes and swallowed hard. I took a few deep breaths before saying, "Am I doing something wrong?"

"What? No." His eyes flew open. "Why would you think that?"

"Because," I said quietly. "We haven't done more than *this* in a month, Grayson." I was choosing my words carefully, fully aware that everyone in the house could hear us.

"You almost died, Isabel. I'm giving you time to heal." He put his hands on my thighs, causing a tremble in my body despite my annoyance with him.

"I've been healed for three weeks," I said firmly. "Try again."

Grayson lifted one hand, running it through his hair. He looked just as beautiful as ever with his rumpled clothes and tousled hair. "I don't know if I can, Isabel."

"I think it's pretty clear you can," I said pointedly.

"That's not what I mean." He sat up and lifted me off him in one smooth motion. Once we were seated next to each other on the edge of the bed, he looked at me with tortured eyes. "When you were dying, there was so much blood. I still don't know how I resisted feeding off you, Isabel."

"But you did," I said.

"Barely. My craving for you was so strong. I thought it would fade after some time, but it hasn't. Most of the time, when I'm with you, it's all I can do to resist the craving." His elbows were on his knees and he dropped his head into his hands. "I want you more than anything, Isabel, but not if it means that I might hurt you."

My hand was shaking as I placed it on his shoulder. I felt terrible for being so oblivious to his pain for the last month. Had I been torturing him just by being around him? How much worse had I made it with my many attempts to seduce him?

"Grayson, why didn't you tell me sooner? I've been torturing you."

"No." His eyes flew to me. "It's not torture, Isabel. Being with you could never be torture for me. It just means I have to be more careful and concentrate on restraint. I can do that."

"For how long?" I asked.

"For as long as I have to." He put a hand on my knee. "I'm sorry, Isabel. I know this isn't fair to you."

"Don't." I shook my head furiously. "You don't get to apologize for this. I'm the reason you even have to worry about this."

He frowned. "It's not your fault either. This is just our situation. We'll adapt."

"Would it help if you drank more blood? From bags, I mean. Would that help control the craving?" I said.

"I've already increased my intake some and it does help. I supposed I could increase it a little more." He didn't sound thrilled by the prospect. When he saw the eager look on my face, he sighed. "You want me to do that right now?"

"One month, Parker," I said with extra emphasis. "It's been one month. I might not be torturing you, but you are most certainly torturing me."

Grayson smiled faintly. "Fine, I'll give it a shot, but you really need to work on your self-control, Jones."

On a whim, I threw my arms around him. Grayson's body went rigid for a second and I worried that I was making things worse, but then he sighed and put his arms around me as he buried his face in my neck.

"Are you sure you don't want to just go to a movie or something tonight?" he said.

"Whatever you want." I closed my eyes and rested my

head on his shoulder. "I'd be perfectly happy just staying like this for the rest of the night."

Grayson pressed his lips lightly against my neck. "I'd be perfectly happy staying like this for the rest of my life."

We stayed that way for a few minutes, until a knock at the door pulled Grayson away. He smoothed down his hair and greeted Trina with a less than enthusiastic hello. She caught my eye and nodded once before asking Grayson to meet with her in the council room. The vampire leadership had been meeting frequently since the disappearance of the town's magic. Grayson updated me occasionally, but I mostly tried to stay out of vampire business. Grayson left without a backward glance and I knew he would be gone for a while. His council meetings were never short these days.

I thought about getting a head-start on my English paper, but my brain was too foggy from the lingering oxytocin to concentrate on dissecting literature. I thought about seeing what Sloan was up to, but she was most likely with Nick and I wasn't ready to be confronted with that new reality yet. I decided to talk a walk through the mansion's garden while there was still a little light left.

Tonight was a full moon and without the magical enchantments, the weres would be forced to turn tonight. They would stay in the woods as much as possible, but I wasn't going to put my trust in a bunch of supernatural wolves. Especially since Dorian had never been shy about his interest in turning me into one of them.

I'd been spending a lot of time in the garden lately, usually waiting for Grayson to wake from his daily vampire comas. A month ago, it had been a mess of weeds and over-grown brush. Once Grayson had learned I was spending my afternoons out there, he had taken the initiative to clean it up. He even helped me transplant some flowers that we both knew wouldn't make it through the winter, but they looked pretty for now and would return again in the spring.

I took a seat on the bench that was still beneath a few rays of fading sunlight. It would be completely dark in less than an hour. Grayson had warned me about a life lived in darkness, but I hadn't been fully prepared for its consequences. While I still lived a normal, daytime life with the other humans, I found myself getting pulled further into the supernatural life. I was staying up late to spend more time with Grayson, making me extra-tired during the day. I was starting to prefer the darkness and that worried me.

"This is a beautiful garden."

I jumped to my feet and whirled. At the edge of the mansion property, right where it reached the wooded land, a woman stood watching me. She was about ten yards away, but even from a distance I could detect her supernatural aura.

"Who are you?" I said as I tried to determine her species.

"I'm Samara," she said. Her voice had a breathy quality. "I'm the leader of the local coven and I'm here because of you, Isabel."

"Me?" I surveyed the trees behind her, checking for other witches. "Did Jane send you?"

She smiled patronizingly. "No, dear. Your mother sent me."

"My mother?" My heart beat faster. I hadn't seen or heard from my mother in ten years. "I don't have a mother."

"We all have a mother, Isabel," Samara said. "Yours has perhaps been absent, but she is still your mother."

"Not to me." I took a step back. "Please leave."

"Don't you want to know where she has been for the last ten years?" Samara's voice grew even softer. "Don't you want to know why she left you?"

I had wanted to know the answer to that question every day for the last ten years, but I wasn't going to let Samara know that. "She left because she didn't want to be a mother anymore. Mystery solved."

"Do you really think it's that simple?" Samara frowned. "Our world is more complex than you could ever imagine. If you come with me now, I can show you."

"Gee, thanks for the offer, but I think I'll pass," I said.

"Don't you want to understand your powers?" She tilted her head and squinted as if examining a squished bug. "Don't you want to know who you truly are?"

Up until a few weeks ago, I'd thought I known exactly who I was. Even if I had come into my Hunter legacy late, I'd adapted to it quickly. But that was before I had discovered that my touch could kill a vampire. Samara understood that power and she could answer the questions I had about my true nature. But there was no way to know if she could be trusted.

"Isabel?"

I whipped around at Grayson's call. He came through the door and stepped onto the stone path that would bring him to the garden. "I'll be right there," I said in a normal tone, knowing that he would be able to hear me. I didn't want him to come close enough to see Samara, but I didn't need to worry because when I turned back to the trees, Samara was gone.

Grayson greeted me with a smile when I met him at the door. He looked more relaxed than he had in his bedroom and asked if I would be up for a stroll. I was nervous about running into Samara again, so I demurred. "It's cold," I said, feigning a chill.

I was rewarded with a skeptical look, but Grayson didn't protest. It wasn't a secret that he would do anything to keep me happy and that only made me feel worse for lying to him. I wasn't sure why I didn't want him to know about Samara, but for now I was going to keep her existence to myself.

One of the vamps was hosting a vampire movie marathon and I was surprised when Grayson suggested we partake. He normally was very good at avoiding parties at the mansion. When we entered the room, everyone looked as surprised as me, but Grayson just led the way to one of the couches. Once we were seated, someone offered him a glass of blood and he took it without hesitation.

I forced my face to remain blank. He was only doing what I had asked by increasing his blood intake. I knew if I had any reaction at all, he might change his mind. The other vampires were all laughing and cheering at the action on television. They were playing a game where they all took a drink anytime a ridiculous vampire stereotype occurred. If I'd been playing along with alcohol, I would have been drunk within thirty minutes.

Grayson wasn't playing along with the others, but he did finish the blood quickly and then placed the empty glass out of sight. Then he surprised me again by putting his arm around my shoulders. We were both laughing along with the others in no time and I almost forgot that I was a human surrounded by a dozen vampires.

The second movie had a lot more dialogue and a lot less action and I found myself dozing off with my head on Grayson's shoulder. I hadn't realized just how tired I was until he put his lips to my ear and said, "Do you want to go to bed, darling?"

I lifted my head and nodded slowly and put my hand on his leg when he started to get up. "You should stay. It's still early."

"I have some work to do anyway," he said with a reassuring smile.

Every eye watched us as we left the room, but Grayson just gave them all a stiff good night and I waved like an idiot. He stopped at his study and I continued on to his bedroom. I wondered if I would ever consider it our bedroom or if it would always feel like his. Half of his closet now held my clothes and my toothbrush had its own spot in the bathroom. My shampoo was in the shower and my towel hung next to his. This was just as much my space as Grayson's, but I still felt like a guest in someone else's home.

After I had stripped out of my own clothes, I pulled on the same t-shirt of Grayson's that I always slept in. I found it both comfortable and comforting, but now I thought about Sloan's comment about sexy lingerie. Given what he had told me earlier, it was probably best that I keep away from seductive clothing.

I came out of the bathroom and pulled up abruptly. Grayson had started a fire and he was looking at me very much like he used to look at me, back when his favorite activity was undressing me.

"What about your work?" I asked.

"Consider this me mixing business and pleasure." He held out a hand and I stepped forward and took it. "I'm not making any promises, Isabel, but I'm willing to try."

"Did the blood help?" I tried not to sound too hopeful.

He nodded. "I can feel a difference. But that might change."

"I understand." I gave him a reassuring smile. "If we have to stop, that's okay."

"It would probably help if you weren't so damn beautiful," he said, stroking my cheek.

"Maybe you should close your eyes," I suggested with a playful smile.

Grayson stared hard into my eyes and my heart fluttered in response. I hadn't thought it was possible, but I found myself falling even more in love with him when he said, "I don't think I can look away from you for even a second."

"Well, you better figure out a way because kissing me with your eyes open is just creepy, Parker," I said, putting my arms around his neck as I pushed up on my toes, bringing me slightly closer to his eye-level.

"Noted." Grayson swooped his head down the remaining few inches and kissed me harder than he had in the last month. I had forgotten just how well he had perfected that skill. In seconds, my whole body was burning with desire. "Are you alright?" he asked when he noticed my body was trembling.

"Yeah," I breathed, sucking in a deep breath. "You?"

"No complaints so far," he said. His hands rested tentatively on my hips. "Let's keep going."

I kissed my way along his jaw, stopping at his ear. My hands were already tugging at the hem of his shirt. "If you insist."

"Hey," Grayson caught both my hands in one of his and used his other hand to cup my chin gently. "However this turns out, I need you to know that I love you and I will never, ever hurt you."

"I know, Grayson." I gently pulled my arms away from his grip and put my palms flat against his chest. "I trust you completely."

17

Grayson had to move slower than usual and some of the unbridled passion had to be dialed back, but we made it through the night with complete success. I knew that it wouldn't have been the end of the world if we'd had to stop, but knowing that Grayson was still able to keep his control with me was an important moment for both of us.

"You can't erase it," I said as Grayson ran his fingers over the scar just above my hipbone for at least the twentieth time. I had thought that I would fall asleep immediately, but I was wide awake now and we were both content to lie entwined in bed, having quiet conversation.

"I'm not trying to erase it," he said, sounding guilty. "Do you realize that's the second scar you have on your body because of him?"

We were talking about Nick again. I sighed. "I thought we had moved past the whole jealousy thing, Grayson."

"I'm not jealous of Nick," Grayson said, letting his hand trail along my hip. "I'm worried about you. You almost died twice to save him and you've told me more than once that you love me more than you ever loved him."

"I do," I said fervently.

"I know. That's why I'm worried." He shifted next to me, bringing his body closer to mine. "I'm worried someday you might die because of me."

"Not because of you," I corrected him. "But I would die *for* you. If there was a chance to save you, I would absolutely sacrifice myself."

"I really wish you wouldn't say that." Grayson was quiet for a long moment. "How would you feel about leaving town with me after you graduate?"

I pushed myself up onto an elbow to see if he was being serious. "Really?"

"Sure, why not?" He smiled adorably. "We've talked about traveling together. It could be fun to see some of the world."

"It could get tricky," I said. "Your sun allergy is going to limit us."

"We'll work around it."

I thought about his offer and it wasn't like I had a better plan. Plus, it would be nice to have some alone time with Grayson where we didn't have dozens of vampires and weres swarming around us. "You might regret your offer after I tell you that I'm actually going to graduate next month. Turns out I have enough credits from my old school to finish a semester early."

"You're going to graduate early?" He raised a curious eyebrow. "Have I been dating a nerd this whole time?"

"Please, let's not pretend that's a shock." I poked him in the side. "Besides, who's the nerd with an entire library in his bedroom?"

"That's just to impress the chicks into sleeping with me," he said smugly as he ran a hand along the length of my body. "It works."

I cocked an eyebrow at him. "Who says I'm impressed?"

"Darling, we both know you were more than impressed by me tonight." He winked playfully and I laughed before leaning in to kiss him. Why did he have to be so utterly irresistible?

"Are you still doing okay?" I asked gently, hesitant to ruin the mood.

"Yeah." His smile reached his eyes, making them flash like the flames in the fireplace. He brushed my hair back and his fingers lingered at my neck. "I'm doing just fine."

"How fine?" I asked in a sultry voice.

Grayson laughed. "Not that fine, Jones. I'm still recharging. We don't all have magical blood in our veins."

His words were meant to be an innocent tease, but I felt like I'd been punched in the gut. Until now, I'd been able to forget about Samara's portentous appearance in the garden. I'd also convinced myself that I was doing the right thing by not telling Grayson. But now, he was looking at me with such pure love that I felt terrible for keeping such a secret from him.

"I need to tell you something," I said, rolling away so we were no longer touching. "I should've told you earlier."

"Okay, that's a little ominous." His smile faded quickly.

"When I was in the garden earlier, I wasn't alone." I sat up, hugging my knees to my chest. Even with the roaring fire, a chill ran through my body. "A woman appeared from the woods. She said her name is Samara and she's the leader of the local coven."

At that, Grayson sat up. "Samara was here? Talking to you?"

"Do you know her?" I reached for the blanket at the foot of the bed and wrapped it around myself, but the chill remained.

"I know of her. Trina has been meeting with Samara regarding the fall's magical depletion. She thinks Samara might be able to help us understand what is happening. If we know that, we might be able to fix it." Grayson looked unconvinced. "What did she want from you?"

I looked toward the fire, watching the crackling embers with rapt attention. It was easier to stare into a raging fire than it was to look into Grayson's eyes as I admitted, "She wanted to take me to my mother."

"Your mother?" Grayson sounded lost when he added, "I thought she was dead."

"Dead?" I whipped my head to him in surprise. "Why did you think that?"

"I don't know." He shrugged. "You've never talked about her. I just assumed she died when you were younger."

I couldn't believe that I had never mentioned my mother to Grayson. I distinctly remembered the day I had told Nick about her abandonment. How had I neglected to mention it to the man I loved?

"Not dead, just absent." I flicked away a stubborn strand of hair that fallen into my eyes. "She left us ten years ago and I haven't heard from her since. Until today."

"She sent Samara?" Grayson guessed. "And you sent Samara away?"

"I have no interest in ever seeing my mother again," I said coldly. "Please don't try to convince me otherwise."

His jaw clenched as he studied me. "Isabel, if anyone can understand how you feel about your mother, it's me."

"She never even reached out to me after my father was murdered." I couldn't keep the emotion out of my voice. The blanket slipped from one shoulder and I shivered harder as cold air hit my exposed skin.

"Alright, maybe I can't completely understand." He put

the blanket back in place on my shoulder and left his hand there. My body instantly stopped shaking. "If you don't want to see her, I support you. But I know you have a lot of questions about your power, and I'd bet she could help answer some of those questions. Don't let your anger at her get in the way of finding some peace for yourself."

"Okay, now I'm impressed." I smiled begrudgingly. "Have you always been this smart and I just didn't notice because I was blinded by your beauty?"

He smirked. "I'm not just a pretty face."

"You really think I should go to her?" I asked, unable to think about anything else now that I'd started the discussion.

"I do." Grayson moved his hand slowly over my back. "I think you'll regret it if you don't at least give her a chance to explain."

"You don't regret seeing Jane?" I asked. "It doesn't bother you knowing that she moved on and started a new family?"

"No. I never assumed her life had stopped when mine did." He tilted his head. "Is that your biggest concern? That she might have started over without you?"

I thought for a second and shook my head. "My biggest concern is that she wishes I had never existed at all."

Grayson pulled me to him, putting his arms around me. "I don't think that will be the case, Isabel, but you'll never know unless you agree to see her one more time. If it will help, I'll go with you."

"It will help," I said with my face buried against his neck, my words muffled. "I don't think I could face her alone."

"You don't have to." He stroked my hair and said, "You'll never be alone again, Isabel. I'm always with you."

Grayson held me for a long time and I was in no rush to push him away. The steady rhythm of his heart was the most calming sound in the world and eventually it lulled me to sleep, but not before I felt his lips against my ear as he whispered. "I love you so much, Isabel. Remember that, always."

An hour before dawn, I woke in Grayson's bed with a pile of blankets wrapped around me. The fire was out, but the room wasn't completely dark. Brilliant moonlight cascaded through the window, bathing Grayson in a way that made it seem like his skin was glowing. He was standing in front of the window, absolutely still.

"Grayson?' I said, wondering if I was dreaming.

"Isabel." He turned, looking stunned. I noticed he had pulled on a pair of black pants, but no shirt. "Something is wrong."

"Wrong?" I shook my head a little to clear the sleep-fog. "What time is it? The moon is so bright."

He walked toward the bed, stopping to scoop up my clothes. As he handed them to me, I noticed he was shaking. "Get dressed, darling."

"What's happening?" I didn't like his worried tone or the way his eyes didn't quite meet mine, but I did as he asked and pulled on my clothes.

Grayson had gone back to the window, his head moving slowly from side-to-side as he scanned the outside. Wolves were howling incessantly in all directions. "That started about an hour ago," he said when I came to stand next to him. "I was sitting here reading when I felt this electric charge in the air and the howling started. Do you feel it?"

I nodded, finally noticing that my skin was tingling in an unpleasant way. "What is that?"

"I don't know." He finally looked at me. "But it's not good. The moon is still high in the sky and it's almost time for the sun to rise."

"We need to find Sloan," I said. "She might be able to

figure out what is causing this. It must be some magical force."

Grayson opened his mouth to say something, but froze. After a long pause, he said, "She's in the mansion...with Nick."

"I know." I grimaced a little. "She told me earlier. How long have you known?"

"I didn't know, until tonight." He gave me a guilty smile. "But I'm not sure I would've told you if I had known."

"I'm not sure I'd have wanted you to tell me," I admitted. "Can you get Nick's attention? I really don't want to walk in on them the way he did with us."

Even Grayson shuddered a little. "Good call."

He called Nick's name in a voice that was just slightly louder than normal and waited for Nick to acknowledge him. After telling Nick to meet us in the kitchen, Grayson lowered his voice and said to me, "They'll be there in a few minutes."

"Is anyone else in the house paying attention?" I said.

"It's still pretty empty." With the vampires being cooped up during the day now, most of them spent their nights away from the mansion. He headed to the door. "Hopefully we'll be able to figure out what is happening before everyone returns."

As we waited in the kitchen for Nick and Sloan, I filled a glass with water and drank it down in two big gulps. When I was done, I took a blood bag from the fridge and poured a few ounces into the glass. Grayson's eyes widened when I handed it to him.

"I think you've exercised enough self-control for one night," I said.

He nodded once and took the glass without protest. That was when I knew how much he must have been struggling to be around me. I walked away, letting him do what he needed to do without worrying about my reaction. The wolves were still howling excitedly and I tried to spot them through the window. My human eyes could only see to the end of the garden, just before it met the woods.

"Do you think this has anything to do with Samara?" I asked.

"It's a strange coincidence if this isn't related to her sudden appearance in the falls." Grayson had finished the blood and he looked slightly more relaxed as he stepped next to me. "I also don't think it's a coincidence this is happening on the night of the full moon."

"Why would anyone want to keep the weres in wolf form?" Unlike vampires, the weres were only deadly when they were in a transitioned state.

"I can't believe I'm going to say this, but I wish Dorian was here so we could ask him." Grayson winced. "Of course, if he was here, I'm sure he would only make snide comments about you just to piss me off."

I smirked. "You really shouldn't let him get to you so easily."

"Are you defending him?" Grayson challenged.

"Dorian? No." I made a disgusted face. "He's cocky, lude, cold, and generally despicable."

Grayson chuckled. "You would've said the same thing about me a couple months ago."

It was true. When I first arrived in the falls, I'd viewed Grayson and Dorian as being very much the same. Both of them had been trying to convince Nick that resisting the transition was pointless. Both of them had enjoyed making me squirm uncomfortably under their penetrating looks and bold words. But I had slowly come to realize that while Dorian was acting purely on selfish, survival instincts,

Grayson was only trying to protect me while having a little fun in the process.

"Dorian just doesn't have your charm," I said, smiling. "Nor your killer smile."

"This smile?" He grinned at me adorably and my heart did a little flip.

"Are you two always this gross?" Sloan asked as she entered the room. Nick trailed behind her look far more sheepish. He wouldn't make eye contact with me.

"Generally, yes," I answered and Grayson laughed softly.

Sloan clapped her hands. "Alright, care to tell us why you pulled us out of bed?"

It was such an honest thing to say, so very Sloan, that I nearly laughed. But I knew that would only make the whole thing even more uncomfortable. I gestured toward the light streaming through the window. "We're less than an hour away from sunrise and the moon is still directly overhead."

"So?" Sloan looked at me like I was crazy, but Nick joined us at the window, squeezing into the small space between us.

"How is that possible?" he asked, staring disbelievingly at the moon. "And what's with all the howling?"

"I suspect the weres are reacting to that electrical charge in the air," Grayson said. "You feel it, don't you?"

Nick nodded. "Yeah. It kind of reminds me of how I used to feel when I swam in the falls before my transition."

"You've felt this before?" Grayson said.

"It's magic," Sloan said calmly. "Really powerful magic. I felt just a twinge of this electricity when Jane and I conjured the protective barrier against Liam's vamps. I thought that was powerful, but it was nothing like this."

"Samara?" I said to Grayson.

He nodded. "Maybe. Seems likely."

"Who is Samara?" Sloan asked.

I frowned. "She's a friend of my mother's, apparently. She also happens to be the local coven's leader and she was lurking in the garden yesterday evening. I don't think that what is happening now is a coincidence."

"Your mother?" Nick's eyes narrowed as he studied me in an unnervingly perceptive way. "I thought you hadn't talked to her in almost a decade."

Without looking at Grayson, I knew that he was glaring at me. It had been one thing that I had neglected to tell him about my mother, but it was so much worse that I had clearly confided in Nick.

"I haven't," I said quietly. "I have no idea why she sent Samara."

"You didn't agree to meet with your mother?" Nick asked.

"No." I turned away from the window and from Nick's concerned face. "I have nothing to say to that woman."

"Iz," Nick reached out a hand and then froze. It was a reflex for him to want to comfort me, but the watchful eyes of Sloan and Grayson snapped him back to reality. He cleared his throat and ran his hand through his hair instead of completing its original journey. "I think this is your mother's way of showing you just what she can do if you don't agree to meet with her."

"She's threatening me?" My stomach tightened into a painful knot. "That doesn't make any sense. Why would she do that?"

Grayson said, "We never found the witch that was working for Liam."

"You think it was my mother?" I gaped at him.

"I don't know, Isabel," he said with a shrug, "but it's a strong possibility."

"I still don't understand why Izzy's mother would threaten her. That doesn't make any sense," Sloan said.

At first, I agreed with her. None of this made any sense. Even if my mother was working with Liam, it didn't make any sense that she had waited a month to make a move on us. It made even less sense that her move was to extend nighttime, a time when the supernaturals would be at their strongest. But the thing that made the least sense was doing any of this to send a message to me.

"Grayson," I said, my eyes widening. "If she can control the moon like this, is it possible she could do the same thing with the sun?"

"She's not controlling the moon," Sloan said. "It's just an aberration. I'm sure the second we leave the town, everything is back to normal. She's just creating an illusion over the falls to make us think it's still night."

"So, she could do the opposite, too? Make it seem like it's daytime all the time?" My heart was beating faster.

Grayson stared at me. "She can use these aberrations to completely control the supernaturals in town."

In a bit of perfect timing, the moonlight outside began to rapidly shift. We all hurried back to the window and watched in awe as the moon dropped quickly in the sky while the sun began to rise over the opposite horizon. The howling began to fade as quickly as the moonlight.

"This can't be good," Nick breathed.

"We finally agree on something," Grayson said wryly. "The others should be back soon. I'll convene the council."

"The council won't be able to stop this," I muttered. "I have to do it."

Grayson shook his head. "No, Isabel. You can't blindly go to a woman you haven't seen in ten years and trust that she won't harm you."

"She's my mother," I said hotly.

"She left you," he said, equally intense as he waved a

hand toward the window. "Look what she is capable of doing."

"Colleen may be crazy, but she's still my mother." I glared at Grayson. "Please don't pretend to know what she is capable of doing to me."

Nick put a hand on Sloan's arm. "Let's go meet the others," he said quietly as he pulled her from the room. She shot me one last sympathetic look before turning to follow him.

"You told Nick about her," he said, as soon as they were gone. We both knew that Nick would still hear everything, but Grayson didn't care. "What else aren't you telling me?"

"Stop it, Grayson." I crossed my arms and fixed a cold stare at him. "You don't get to turn this into something it isn't. I didn't tell you about my mother because I don't like talking about her. Nick knows about her because he asked me about her. If you had asked me, I would have told you."

His flinch was undeniable. "Is that how our relationship works? I have to ask you everything or you won't tell me anything?"

"Why are you being like this?" I demanded.

"How would you feel if I hadn't told you about my mother before we met her? Would you have been completely comfortable learning about my past in front of other people?" His jaw twitched as he looked at me, a poor attempt to hide his emotion.

"No, I wouldn't have liked that," I said in a calmer voice. "I wasn't trying to keep anything from you. I'm sorry."

He nodded, once. "I know. I'm not mad at you. I think I'm mad at myself for never even bothering to ask you about her. I'm sorry. I've been a pretty shitty boyfriend."

"No, you haven't." I put a hand to my side, over the skin that was still a little tender. "You saved my life, Grayson."

"I would have done that even if we'd never gotten together, Isabel. That had nothing to do with me being your boyfriend," he said, still looking pained. "Do you realize that I don't know anything about you before you came to the falls? You never told me about that Steve guy. I bet Nick knew about him."

I looked away, too ashamed to answer. "It doesn't matter," I said. "My past doesn't matter. I'm not that girl anymore."

"Because that girl never would have been with a vampire?" he guessed. "Is that why you keep me at a distance? Because some part of you thinks our relationship is wrong."

"Grayson, I'm not ashamed of us." I wasn't in the mood to indulge in his pity party. "But if you're asking me if I always wanted to date a vampire, the answer is no."

"Well, that works out well considering I never wanted to *be* a vampire." He scoffed and looked away.

Sunlight had started to replace the moonlight coming through the window, and it was only a matter of time before Grayson and the other vamps would be hunkering down for the day. I didn't have a lot of time left to convince him. "Listen to me, Grayson Parker." I grabbed his shirt and pulled hard until he was close enough for me to put my arms around him. "I might not have wanted to fall in love with a vampire, but I absolutely wanted to fall in love with you. *You* are the person I always wanted to be with, it just took me a while to figure it out."

"Too long," he said, dropping his head down to meet mine. "I wish that you could've known me before all this."

"You do realize that I was, like, 12 when you were still human." I laughed as he groaned. "For what it's worth, I'm sure 12-year-old Isabel Jones would've had a huge crush on 17-year-old Grayson Parker."

"This conversation has taken a strange turn," Grayson said with an awkward laugh. "Can we go back to you telling me how much adult-Isabel adores me?"

"More than anything in this world, that's how much." As I stretched my head up to kiss him, I made up my mind about what I would do next. We couldn't let my mother continue to manipulate the falls, and the supernatural creatures that lived there, even if that meant I had to meet with her.

"You alright?" Grayson asked when he noticed how my body tensed.

"Yeah." I forced a smile. "Your vamps are back. We should probably disengage."

He kissed me one more time and stepped back. "I need to go take care of things. Will you be here when I'm done? We can talk more about how to deal with your mother."

"Do what you need to do. We'll talk later." I kept the smile on my face a beat too long and he froze at the doorway.

"Don't sneak off, okay?" he said, looking worried. "I've got this weird feeling you are going to disappear on me."

"Don't be so paranoid," I said with a laugh that rang hollow.

Grayson continued to stare at me, looking very much like he didn't trust anything I was saying. But the vamps down the hall were getting louder and he had a job to do. "I love you, Isabel," he said, not caring if they overheard him.

"I love you, too," I replied immediately.

Logically, I knew it was impossible that he had read my mind, but the look he gave me made it seem as though he knew exactly what I had just decided. I waited a few minutes after he was gone before opening the back door and stepping outside. It was cold and I wished I'd thought to grab my jacket, but that would've only heightened Grayson's suspicions.

At the edge of the garden, I returned to the spot where Samara had approached me. I had no idea if she would be waiting for me, but my gut told me that if I waited long enough she would come for me. "Let's get this over with, Samara," I said out loud with a sigh.

She appeared so suddenly, I felt I must be hallucinating. "You called?" Samara said, looking ethereal as she glided out of the trees in her flowing gown.

"I'll go with you to meet my mother," I said.

"You will?" She looked surprised. "She will be pleased to see you."

"Whatever." I wasn't in the mood for small talk. "How do we do this? Is she in town or do we need to fly there on a broom or what?"

Samara smirked. "You make witches sound so primitive."

"You'll have to forgive me. My mother abandoned me as a kid so I don't know a lot about your kind." I was already regretting my decision.

"I'm surprised the vampire is letting you do this," she said, ignoring my sassy remark. "He doesn't strike me as someone who would trust the witch coven."

"Grayson isn't in charge of me. I make my own decisions." I didn't think she needed to know that I was technically sneaking away without telling him. "He is right not to trust you, though. We don't know anything about you."

"You know that I am working with your mother. That should be enough." Samara stepped closer and held out her hand. "Give me your hand, Isabel. It's time to go."

I stared at her hand and debated whether I should take it. Samara couldn't be trusted simply because she knew my mother, especially considering I didn't trust my mother at all. She'd done nothing to show that she was worthy of my trust.

In the end, I didn't have a choice. I had to see my mother and convince her to stop engaging in magical warfare. As I reached out to take Samara's hand, I heard a loud crash from the mansion and turned in time to see Grayson's angry face. "Isabel, don't!"

For just a second, I froze. Was I about to make a terrible mistake? Grayson sure seemed to think so. But before I could change my mind, Samara's hand closed hard around my wrist and she muttered a few words in a language I didn't understand. The air around us swirled a hazy shade of blue before turning bright white. I found Grayson's face one more time through the fog and then he was gone and I was, too.

Continued in Book Four: DEMONS AT DUSK

Sign up for E.J.'s Mailing List.
You'll receive information about new releases and sales, plus a bunch of free books just for signing up!

ABOUT THE AUTHOR

E.J. King is a dreamer and a storyteller. She combines these two loves to spin engaging, wild stories. She's an avid reader of all types of genres and writes what she loves to read. E.J. writes contemporary romance, urban fantasy, romantic thrillers, and paranormal stories.

Her urban fantasy/ paranormal romance series "Dark Souls," has six books and two short stories to date and more on the way. She is also the author of two other paranormal/urban fantasy series. "The Blackwood Vampires" is set in the Dark Souls world and "Shadow Hunters" explores a new world of monsters and hunters.

For a full list of all E.J. King books and links to buy, go to: E.J.'s BOOKS

Sign up for E.J.'s Mailing List.
You'll receive a free starter library just for signing up!

Keep reading for an excerpt from
DEMONS AT DUSK

CHAPTER ONE

W hen the fog cleared, I was no longer in the garden. In fact, I was sure I wasn't in Shaded Falls anymore. Samara had used her powers to teleport us far away from Grayson and the mansion. I looked around, surprised to see that Samara was already walking across the open field where we had landed.

"Where are we?" I asked, hurrying to catch up with her.

"Your mother is staying in the house just across the street," Samara said without slowing down to wait for me.

"You couldn't just teleport us into her house?" I said.

"Teleporting requires a witch to draw on elements from nature. That is easiest to do when one is outside." Samara marched directly across the street, not even pausing to check for traffic. I followed closely while trying to take in every detail of our new location. The house we were approaching was similar to Sloan's home.

The teleportation had left me feeling queasy and slightly dizzy. I couldn't deny that it was an efficient way to travel, however. I wondered if Samara had to know the exact location of where she was traveling, how far she could teleport, and if she could also jump through time? There was still so much about the mystical world that I didn't understand.

"Is this my mother's house?" I asked skeptically. It was such a normal looking home that it was hard to picture my mother living there, carrying out her magical manipulations. "This doesn't look like a house that would entice Hansel and Gretel."

"You have a warped view of witches," Samara said. "We would never harm innocent children."

"Except your own?" I said with a snarl, thinking of my mother.

Samara had already disappeared into the house and I followed reluctantly. I wasn't ready to see my mother, but there was no point dragging out the torture. When Samara led me into a large room with a group of women seated around a circular table, I recognized Colleen immediately. She looked exactly the same as the day that she left our home for the last time. Samara took the empty chair next to her.

"Isabel, darling," she said, rising from her chair.

"Don't call me that," I snapped harshly. That wasn't a word I wanted to hear in her voice. It was Grayson's term of endearment for me and I didn't want to associate it with my mother. "Don't."

Colleen made no reaction other than to wave a hand toward the lone empty chair. "Please, have a seat."

"Just like our old family dinners," I said as I begrudgingly slid into the chair. "Minus the father figure, of course."

"I was very sorry to hear about your father," Collen said in a cold voice.

"Why do I find that hard to believe?" I muttered.

The other women in the room were thoroughly enter-

E.J. KING

tained by our family drama, their eyes bouncing back-and-forth between us like they were watching a tennis match.

"Isabel, we can either spend this time listening to your abandonment issues or we can get to the point." Colleen glared at me the same way she used to when I would misbehave as a child. "Surely you want to know why I sent for you."

She had a point, but I wasn't ready to capitulate just yet. "I would've preferred if you had just come for me yourself. Teleportation isn't easy on the stomach."

"You get used to it." Colleen looked down at the table and for the first time, I noticed the map spread in front of her. "You were only teleported a hundred miles. It's much worse over longer distances."

"I'll keep that in mind." The other women were studying me so closely it was all I could do not to crawl under the table. "Why am I here, Colleen?"

"I'm afraid you aren't going to like the reason." Her brown eyes were dark, nearly black, when she looked at me. "The coven has found a way to end the vampire threat, but we need your assistance."

"End the vampire threat?" My heart beat loudly in my chest. "What does that mean?"

Samara leaned forward, a delighted twinkle in her eye. "We can eliminate them. No more vampires."

"What?" There was a dull ringing in my ears. My mother and her coven were planning to kill the vampires. "You can't do that."

"We can and we will." Colleen lifted an eyebrow, surprised by my horrified reaction. "I can understand your reluctance to help me, but surely you can agree that eliminating the vampire bloodline is a worthwhile endeavor."

"Isabel has been cohabitating with a vampire clan in the

falls," Samara explained with a smirk. "It appears she is in love with one of them."

"In love with a vampire?" one of the other women said with a gasp.

Colleen's eyes narrowed. "Is this true, Isabel?"

"Yes." I stared back at her without flinching. "My boyfriend is a vampire. My friends are vampires and werewolves and even a witch. I have no interest in killing any of them."

"Vampires and werewolves are a violation of nature," Collen said coldly. "If you keep associating with them, they will kill you."

"Grayson would never hurt me," I said defiantly. "He saved my life more than once."

"Would your life have even been in danger if it wasn't for him?" she guessed astutely.

I struggled to stay calm. "My life was in danger long before I met Grayson Parker. Maybe if my mother had bothered to warn me about my heritage, I might have been able to protect myself."

"If vampires didn't exist, you would never have needed to protect yourself." Colleen's expression was cold and smug. "Vampires killed your father. He's dead because of them, not me. How could you befriend those creatures and yet regard me with such contempt?"

"Because they didn't choose to be vampires, but you chose to abandon your family." I wanted to storm away from the table, but I had nowhere to go. I still didn't even know where I was. "I'm not going to help you kill my friends. If that was the only purpose of this meeting, we can adjourn now."

"You have a skewed view of supernatural beings. Shaded Falls has been a haven, protecting you from some harsh realities. Now that the protective barrier has fallen, their true natures will begin to show." Colleen's eyes darted to Samara. "Has order been restored to the falls?"

"Yes." Samara nodded her head once. "The sun will keep the town safe for now."

"Wait, are you the ones that removed the protective barrier?" I looked at each woman and noted they had the same cocky look as Samara. "Why would you do that? The humans in the falls were safe. Now, you've put them in danger."

Colleen cleared her throat, directing my eyes back to her. "The spell that protected the humans was taken down to convince Liam that we were on his side. It had to be done for us to achieve our end goal."

"You were the witch working with Liam? Why would you do that?" I could feel anger and bile rising in my throat. "Liam wanted to drain my blood."

"I needed to become friends with your enemy. It was the only way to verify my theory about your powers. I needed to see you kill a vampire, so I manipulated the vampire you wanted dead more than anything." Colleen sounded slightly proud of her evil plan. "You were never truly in danger. I was never going to let him hurt you."

"And yet, I almost died." I could practically feel my scar burning.

"Your actions that night could not have been predicted." She flapped a hand in the air like she was flicking away my words. "That was an incredibly dangerous and stupid thing to do, Isabel."

I laughed. "You helped a vampire attack me and my friends, but I'm the stupid one? Drop dead, Colleen."

"If you want to hate me, fine. I can understand that. But you can't honestly tell me that you think humanity would be better off if we continued to let vampires prowl in the darkness." She frowned at me. "Remove your personal feelings from this conversation. You can't truly feel that vampires should exist when they pose such a threat to humanity."

"Humans also pose a threat to humanity," I said. "How about we just get rid of all the humans, too?"

"You are being unreasonable," she said with a disappointed shake of her head. I had a flashback to my childhood when she had made that exact disapproving reaction after catching me coloring on the walls of my childhood bedroom. "We can stop the vampires without you, Isabel. It will be more difficult, but we will still succeed."

I swallowed hard, cowed by the certainty of her words. "Why am I here, Colleen? If you can do this without me, why did you bring me here?"

"Because if you aren't going to work with us, I need to make sure you won't be working against us." Colleen exchanged another look with Samara. It was almost like they were having a conversation without using words. "Isabel, I can't make you join the coven. You have to make that choice of your own volition. But I'm not going to let you interfere in our efforts to make the world a better place."

"A better place?" I laughed. "You have a lot of nerve claiming the moral high ground when your plan is to kill a bunch of innocent people who haven't hurt anyone."

I shoved away from the table and jumped to my feet. I'd given Colleen enough of my time. I still had no idea where I was or how I would make it back to the falls, but I couldn't stay in the same house as her any longer. None of the witches tried to stop me as a raced toward the front door. My hand closed around the doorknob and I yanked hard, gasping when the door didn't budge. I checked to make sure it wasn't locked and tried again, but the door stayed firmly shut.

"What is this?" I demanded, trying yet again.

"It's been spelled," Samara said softly. She had followed me to the door. "You can try every door and window in this house, but none of them will open for you."

"You've trapped me in here?" I growled.

"It's for your own good," Samara said. "It is too dangerous to have you out there while we are making preparations for tomorrow night."

I kicked the door and relished the sharp pain that shot through my foot. At least I still had control of my body even if I couldn't make it leave the house. "What's tomorrow night?"

"We will perform the ritual." Samara didn't wait around for me to ask questions. She was gone before I could even open my mouth.

Despite her warning, I attempted to open the door at least a dozen more times before moving to the windows. They were sealed tightly shut no matter how hard I tried to shove them open.

"Let me out!" I yelled, banging on the window pane.

"You're only going to hurt yourself," a quiet voice said.

I turned and appraised the young girl staring at me. She had been seated next to Samara at the table. "You'll understand if I choose not to listen to one of my captors, right?"

"I'm Emma," the girl said with a small smile. "I'm sorry we had to take such drastic measures. I'm hopeful you won't hold it against us for long."

"Why, do you want us to be best friends?" I glared at her.

Emma shrugged. "You are stuck here either way, Isabel. If you are smart, you'll make the best of it."

"How old are you?" I asked abruptly.

"I'm 18." She frowned at me. "As you know, no one can join a coven until they are 18."

"I don't know anything about covens," I snapped. "This is not my world, Emma."

She shrugged. "It is now. Besides, aren't you dating a vampire? Covens are a lot safer than vampire boyfriends, Isabel."

"But not nearly as sexy," I said. "What is the ritual?"

"The ritual is an ancient ceremony the coven will perform to draw energy from nature. The more witches that participate in the ritual, the more energy we will be able to draw forth." Emma flipped her nearly-white hair over her shoulder. "It's a very powerful and spiritual experience."

"What does the coven plan to do with all this spiritual energy?" I could hear the other witches roaming around the house, some of them lurking just outside the room.

"You heard what Colleen said." Emma lifted her chin stubbornly. "We are going to eliminate the vampire bloodline."

"You're going to kill my friends," I corrected her.

Emma just shook her head, clearly frustrated by my lack of enthusiasm for the coven's plans. "Look, your mother asked me to show you to your room. Are you going to come peacefully or do I need to spell you?"

I didn't need to ask what she meant by spelling me. I could assume it mean she would force me with magic and I had no desire to experience that. "Fine, show me."

The house was even larger than it had looked from the outside. As Emma led me around the second floor, I counted at least ten bedrooms. My room was to be the one at the end of the hall, not for privacy but because I would have to sneak past all the other witches if I tried to escape.

The second Emma walked away, shutting the door

behind her, I raced to the window. Just like the windows downstairs, it was bolted shut by magic. I groaned and banged my head against the cool glass. With a start, I reached into my back pocket and grabbed my cell phone. I couldn't believe I hadn't thought to use it until now.

My first thought, as always, was Grayson. All I wanted was to hear his voice, but I had no idea what I would say to him. I had chosen to come with Samara, after all. I had chosen to leave Grayson, despite his request that I not do anything reckless. If I called him, I had no doubt that he would do everything in his power to find me. It would be too dangerous for him show up here. I had to protect him from the coven, and that meant I had to stay. I would find out how they planned to eliminate the vampires and I would stop them. I would find a way to keep Grayson safe, even if that meant killing my own mother.

Made in the USA
Las Vegas, NV
10 January 2022

41066493R00132